Ken Ward was born in 1960. He started to write seriously in 2008, when he joined a writing group. Following a short story being published in a magazine, he developed his character D.I Ray Keane. There have been three books following the policeman, *Time for Revenge* is the latest and he feels there are lots of ideas to continue with. Ken lives in Norfolk with his wife, Jan, and two poodles that keep him company while writing.

Ken Ward

For Jan, always there with a smile and words of encouragement.

Ken Ward

TIME FOR REVENGE

AUSTIN MACAULEY PUBLISHERS™

LONDON • CAMBRIDGE • NEW YORK • SHARJAH

A CIP catalogue record for this title is available from the British Library.

ISBN 9781398451315 (Paperback)
ISBN 9781398451322 (ePub e-book)

www.austinmacauley.com

First Published 2022
Austin Macauley Publishers Ltd®
1 Canada Square
Canary Wharf
London
E14 5AA

Writing is a solitary experience, as it is just me sat at the computer telling the story; as the words build, I get joined by my characters. It is a help as I discuss the progress of the story with friends and even though they may not realise it, just by talking about how I am getting along helps form more ideas for the reader. So, thanks go to Carole and Dan who, over the time this book has taken, have listened to me explaining the process. Thanks also to people who via social media have encouraged me to keep writing as they want to know what is in store for the characters. Thank you to Marina and Rib who were a big help in coming up with the front cover.

Thank you to everyone at Austin Macauley for the work to get this book out there, and all the readers who enjoy a good story.

Chapter One

As the music came from the CD player, Ray Keane couldn't help but pick up the beat and his feet started to move in time with it. He was painting a door frame and found it hard to remember the last time he had felt this relaxed. He turned as he heard Jenny Woods giggle to herself, and saw her standing with coffee in her hand and the widest smile on her face. It was something he had noticed very early in their relationship that when she smiled it lit up her whole face. He realised she had been watching him and in particular his feet,

'I know what you are thinking, and even I surprise myself sometimes when I feel my feet move.'

'Yes, but that is what happens once the dancing bug gets hold of you.'

She stepped forwards and leant in for a kiss then moved back quickly as he brought the paintbrush up towards her nose.

'The paint is meant to go on the woodwork, not me.'

'I know but I think I can spare a small amount.'

They had moved into the house three days ago and as the move had been finalised; Ray had finished up his last case which had been known as a Knife of Honour involving Ben Oakwood and Martin Black. It had worked right for Ray to take some time off. Jenny had also been able to get five days off so their plan was to get as much of the decorating done, and get all their furniture in during this time. Ray had made the point as well the previous evening that it would be nice on the following day to do things together then get ready to go dancing, without having to get away from work first. They drank their coffee and got back to the painting.

They both felt it was lucky for them, that apart from a small amount of painting the rest of the house was reasonable enough to just put in the furniture; they could finish decorating as they wished. Ray had managed to get some of the people from the station who had days off to help with moving stuff in. Jenny had taken the opportunity to invite her parents up and they would give them a hand. Ray had noticed that as he got older, having been told it many times that time did seem to pass quicker. This was even more apparent whenever he had time to spend with Jenny. Before they had time to realise it the afternoon had passed, and they had to get cleaned up and make their way to dancing. When she had first got him interested in dancing, Jenny had suggested they went for lessons at the same classes she attended. This became their routine that once a week they spent a couple of hours at CJ Dance studios; where under the expert eye of Carole, the owner and her tutors Terry and Val, Ray had first built up his confidence to dance, then added steps to each dance. Carole had taken all her dance exams and was the sort of teacher who made learning interesting. Terry along with his wife Lynda enjoyed dancing and was in the process of taking his dance exams, and had helped make Ray feel welcome from the minute he first entered the studio as he was not aware of it but suddenly, he had realised how nervous he felt. Val had the experience of the fact that her parents had taught dancing and it was natural for her as she learnt to dance that she was able to help others learn. The steps he learnt were then practised whenever the chance to attend a dance became available. Ray had always felt that ballroom dancing was a bit starchy, mainly due to only seeing it performed at official events he attended through work.

Carole and the others had shown that dancing was fun and to be enjoyed. He even found that it had made the recent official occasions bearable by being able to participate in the dancing.

When they arrived at the dance studio, there were the usual people to say hello to and as seemed to happen most weeks there were a couple of beginners who always appreciated being made welcome. Ray would make a point of talking to newcomers as he remembered how he had felt on his first night even with Jenny being with him, he had found that he was put at ease by others making him feel welcome. The music started up and Ray was comfortable enough to be the first on the floor as he whisked Jenny around to a quickstep; this was one dance that Ray had taken to and he always enjoyed it. A few of the others joined them on the dance floor and everyone was in a relaxed mood and ready for the lesson to begin. Ray had always enjoyed learning and he found the way Carole taught made it seem easier, each week there would be new steps to learn, and then over the following weeks they would be revised. Slowly these steps became second nature and the class would dance them without thinking. One thing that surprised Ray was how much he had enjoyed dancing from the first lesson, and he could see the same reaction in the faces of the others. He has always enjoyed learning something new, so found new steps a challenge but one that he relished. Carole would have to point out sometimes that he had to give things time; as he grew more confident, he was frustrated if a new step didn't always work out. The lesson soon came to an end, and after saying their goodbyes Ray and Jenny made their way home. It had only been a few days but already going into the house felt right and Jenny asked what he was thinking,

'It does feel like home.'

'Yes, I know, it feels like something I have waited a long time for but it has been worth the wait.'

As was usual after an evening dancing Ray was hungry, and he also had to let the enthusiasm that he always felt calm down. He made some toast and a coffee; while Jenny changed into a dressing gown which she called her comfy clothes. They sat and ate while a programme was on in the background on the T.V. Normally Ray would prefer to have music on but the T.V was a good way to unwind.

'Well as always time seems to have flown, so I have to get ready for work tomorrow.'

Jenny smiled,

'I have two more days before that, with Mum and Dad, I will unpack some more.'

'At least you will not have so far to travel to work from now on. I have just got to get used to a commute again.'

Having wound down after dancing, Ray put the cups in the kitchen and they went to bed. As they walked up the stairs, he couldn't resist giving Jenny a pat on the bottom, she laughed and ran up the last few steps. Ray caught hold of her in the doorway and picked her up, they tumbled onto the bed. It had taken time for him to get used to the feelings he had for

Jenny and especially when they were in bed; he had learnt to relax and go along with these feelings. The laughter eased and they slowly made love. Afterwards, Ray fell into a relaxed sleep and the next thing he knew the alarm was disturbing the peace. He got out of bed and went to make coffee he brought one up to Jenny and kissed her goodbye, she looked at him from under the duvet,

'See you later.' Then she laughed, 'I will have your dinner waiting for you.'

This was something that would not happen as neither of them knew what time Ray would finish. Meals were planned but only cooked once they were both at home.

Ray made the journey into work with a feeling of anticipation that he had not had for a long time. It had been a while since he had had this amount of time off in one go. During his time in the force, work had always been his priority; when he had first joined like a lot of new recruits, he wanted to impress his superiors. Then once he settled in and felt he could be good at the job he wanted to progress through the ranks. During his marriage to Mary, she had supported him and liked it when he did well, so was happy with whatever hours he worked. As the years passed it reached a point where his feelings were that getting the right result was all that mattered, hence his nickname which he knew about but no-one ever used in front of him; this was mustard so he was known to be as Keane as Mustard. Since being with Jenny his priorities had changed, and though he would never let his work suffer he was now willing to let others do some of the tasks he would normally have done. The other element that altered his thinking now was that he was happy with his position in the force. Whenever promotion was mentioned, it was always followed by the comment that he would have more time at his desk to complete paperwork; this would be while others were out at whichever crime scene was being investigated. This thought horrified Ray as he couldn't imagine spending any longer on paperwork than he currently did. He was fit enough to do the job and at his recent medical, the doctor had commented on how well he was looking. It had been important to Ray to keep fit but time always played a part in not allowing him to spend as much time as he would have liked on this aspect. The dancing had been a help in that along with Jenny watching their diet and the exercise he had lost a stone in weight. Ray was happy as a D.I. and saw no reason to alter things. He smiled to himself as he thought that as a D.I. he could still annoy Superintendent Adam Church to a point.

After the 30-minute journey which had not been too bad for traffic, he pulled the car into a parking spot behind the police station.

As he walked in the usual team were behind the front desk, and this was the main reason Ray was happy at King's Lynn in that the team were constant and he knew this showed in their work.

'Morning Jim, how are things?'

'Morning Ray not too bad it has been relatively quiet.'

He carried on through to the C.I.D room where D.C Tim Jarvis was at his desk.

'Morning Tim, where is everyone?'

'Sheila and a couple of the others are out on a first look at some burglaries that took place overnight. There seems to have been a spate of them around the shopping centre within 48 hours.'

This was the quieter aspect of the job, but the one thing Ray instilled in his team was they gave just as much effort to this work as they would a more serious case.

'How is the new house, Ray?'

'Yes, it is fine thanks; Jenny has a few more days to finish unpacking. Anything else happened while I've been off.'

'Not much it has given the team a chance to catch up with things, which seems a rare occurrence recently.'

It had been hectic recently with three high-profile cases occurring quickly after each other. Ray went into his office and even if it had been quieter, there still seemed to be a pile of paperwork on his desk. As much as he detested this side of the job, he decided that the sooner he made a start the better. He poured himself a coffee and slowly started working through things. Two pieces of correspondence grabbed his attention, the first was from a doctor to let him know that a physiological evaluation of Margaret O'Conner was going to take place for the doctors to decide where she would be transferred to for the rest of her sentence. In that he knew she needed medical help his concern was that she may convince people that she should get a chance for parole, when the judge had passed the sentence of life imprisonment, he had recommended it should be a whole of life sentence. The second letter was on a happier note it was from Jeremy Oakwood to let Ray know that his son Ben had been assessed by the team from Combat Stress and they were going to embark on a course of treatment. Even though it was early days, they were optimistic that Ben could return to the army but it would take time and patience for all concerned. As Ray put his signature on another expenses form from one of his officers, the noise level in the office went up as D.S. Sheila

Carr and the others returned from the burglary. Initially, Ray had not been sure how things would go when Jenny transferred but they both knew it was the only way for their relationship to develop. After his first meeting with Sheila, he was apprehensive, but she had shown during the recent case just how capable she was and had fitted in well.

'Hello, Sir, how did you get on with the decorating?'

Ray preferred it if his team called him by his name, but Sheila still seemed to prefer to call him Sir. She had explained that it was just her way; he now didn't correct her anymore.

'Yes, fine thanks, we are just about there now. Is there anything you feel I need to know?'

'Not really these burglaries seem to be following a pattern; that has been reported from other forces in the county. They seem to make a lot of mess which is inconvenient to everyone; they only steal one or two high price items, then after a couple of nights causing chaos, they move on.'

'Adam won't like that. What are we doing about it?'

'Last night was the second night the town has been targeted so I will get extra coverage from uniform and also put a couple of the team out tonight. It just depends how long they stay around for.'

'Ok any CCTV coverage?'

'No, the cameras in the areas so far have not been working.'

This seemed to have been a problem recently that cameras that had been fitted to increase security were not all being used because of council financial cutbacks.

'Right, I will leave that with you but if you need any help then let me know. I better go and see what Adam has to say about it all.'

If ever Ray was pleased to be disturbed by the phone it was if he was due to see Adam. He picked up the ringing phone it was the desk sergeant who told him he had a call from a Constable on duty in Terrington St Clement. This was one of the villages six miles away from Lynn along the A17. At first, Ray didn't understand why a Constable on duty was ringing him. But as he listened to the call it became clear.

Chapter Two

On the other end of the line was P.C. John Ford, who was described by everyone who knew him as old school. He was approaching his 25th year in the force and had never shown any interest in being anything other than a constable. John always enjoyed being out on the beat, this did help him in that he was the sort of policeman who was able to cover the outlying villages, and he had got to know everyone around as they had got to know him. Because of this knowledge when he had responded to the call out, he knew the best person to tell first was Ray.

The 999 calls had come through 45 minutes previously and John took the radio message as he was driving out to cover his mornings beat in Terrington St Clement. The local postman who like John knew the majority of people that he delivered post to, had noticed the post box he used outside the house in Churchgate Way had not been emptied for the last two days. Knowing Steve Edwards, he had walked around the house and had seen no sign of life; if Steve was going to be away for any length of time, he cancelled his post along with other deliveries. John tried the catch on the back gate and it opened easily. He walked onto the patio area and called out Steve's name. Steve had lived in the house for 35 years and it was obvious to anyone that he enjoyed his gardening. As the postman turned around, he saw the legs of someone protruding amongst the roses. He went over and even though he wouldn't have described himself as squeamish; when he saw the injury to the back of the person's head, he promptly left his breakfast in the flower bed. He went back to the patio and fell onto a chair, after a moment to calm his breathing, he used his mobile to call 999; putting into action the next few hours of work.

John Ford knew Steve Edwards well as until eight years ago he had been a D.I. with Norfolk Police. He was also aware that 15 years ago when Ray Keane had joined the station, Steve had taken him under his wing and as well as colleagues they had become friends.

'Hello John; what are you ringing me for?'

'I thought you were the best person to hear this first, I got a call this morning. When I arrived here it is Steve Edwards' house and he was flat out in the flower bed with his skull smashed in.'

It took a lot to shake Ray but this news did. Just before his time off Ray had spoken to Steve on the phone and he still had the note on his desk to ring him and confirm when they could meet up for a chat.

'Right, John, I know I don't need to tell you what to do, but just don't touch anything and I will be there in 15 minutes.'

It was always the same for Ray as a call came in there was a rush of adrenalin that he knew would stay with him through an investigation; but it was joined by a hint of sadness that another life had been extinguished. He moved through the main office and called out,

'Sheila, you are with me; Tim phone Graham, then Lisa and get them out to Churchgate Way in Terrington St Clement. You come out once they are on their way.'

Graham Key was a local doctor, who worked with the police; he was also the pathologist for the area. Even when it was obvious, that someone was dead the police still needed to have a doctor confirm death. Lisa Hall was part of the forensics team and they would scour the crime scene for any clues. The procession of cars had all arrived at the house within 20 minutes of Ray having hung up the phone.

John Ford met Ray at the gate that led to the rear of the house, once Ray had a quick look at the body, he could understand why the postman who was still sat on a patio chair was looking so pale. Two other uniformed officers who had been on patrol on the A17 when they heard the call had also arrived. Ray went over to them,

'Right, you two start an initial house to house, and ask people if they have noticed anything, in particular from what I know so far, we are interested in the last 48 hours.'

Graham had arrived at the house, Ray spoke to Sheila,

'You have a quick word with the postman and get some contact details, then get him home. I will see what Graham can tell us.'

Ray approached the flower bed and Graham spoke first;

'Before you ask, he has been dead for about 48 hours.'

'That is really helpful as the postman has already told us the post has not been taken in for two days.'

Graham smiled as he replied;

'I know, I had heard.'

Some people found these small moments of humour tactless, but they were necessary as a release valve to the pressure that trauma caused.

I can tell you that the skull is a mess, I will have a better look once we move the body; but as always, I will be able to give you more once I do a post mortem.'

They both stepped away as Lisa and her team did a survey of the area around the body.

While they were waiting Graham said,

'By the way Ray, Stephen at the museum phoned to let me know that Ben Oakwood has given the museum the knife he brought back from Bosnia.'

'At least some people will be happy to see the knife.'

As Ray finished speaking Lisa indicated that she had finished her preliminary search, with the body where it was found, so Graham could now have the body moved and the forensic team would continue. As people stood around respectfully while the body was moved Ray thought about what Graham had just told him; the knife that Ben had led to him being treated as a major suspect in a murder case. Ray felt that donating it to the museum was a good step forward in helping him move on with his life. His next thought was where they would start with this investigation; the start of any murder case was always difficult. The first few hours were important as the information they received was from people who had things fresh in their minds. This case was more awkward for Ray as he knew the victim personally.

D.I. Steve Edwards had played a big part in the early career of Ray, policing had changed drastically over the last 27 years since Ray had joined as a cadet. It had altered even more since Steve was a constable. Fortunately to the benefit of Ray, Steve had accepted all the changes and was willing to pass on his knowledge.

Once the body had been removed, Graham left telling Ray he would ring him later with a time for the post mortem. Lisa split her team which consisted of herself and four others into two groups. She and two others concentrated on the garden and in particular the area where the body had been found, the other two went into the house along with several C.I.D officers to see if anything could be discovered. It was obvious that whoever had committed the crime, had only one thought in mind as the patio doors were unlocked but inside it looked as though nothing had been disturbed. Ray decided that the team were capable of dealing with the scene and felt he would be of better use back at the station. He needed to let Adam know the latest and he wanted to get an incident room organised. Before he left, he went to tell John Ford what he required from him next.

'John as soon as things are cleared up here initially; I want you to arrange a room at the village hall that we can use as an incident room.'

John knew how Ray worked so was surprised by this,

'Do you think we will need one here as well as at the station?'

'I think given the situation and until we have more details, it may lead to information coming forward easier from locals. People may be happier speaking to you here also.'

John could see the logic in this and he understood about people being happier talking direct to him as he was well known to them. As they both moved out to the front of the property, John got asked a question he would hear a lot over the next few days. It was from an elderly lady who lived a few doors from the victim.

'Hello Alice, how are you?'

'I am alright John, but how safe should I feel?'

It was amazing how quickly news spread, especially in a village.

'You will be safe, Alice, and you know I will always keep an eye on you.'

Ray was able to see first-hand how the lady relaxed while she was talking to John, even though he knew how good John was at his job he was impressed to see this.

'John, I will speak to you later and also let you know the results of the post mortem, as they may help you out here.'

He left John dealing with two other elderly locals who were expressing their feelings at what they had just heard. The one thing that still surprised Ray was how quickly the press got hold of a story. As he walked back to his car a reporter from the local paper the Lynn News called out to him,

'D.I. Keane, what can you tell us about what is happening here?'

'At the moment nothing at all. Once we have things in place you will get a press release to use.'

'You know we go to print tomorrow, so can't you give us a by-line that we can at least get in that copy.'

'I will get an officer to contact you this afternoon with a piece for you, and that is all I have to say on the matter.'

The reporter was quick enough to know that all that would happen if he pushed the issue was, he would upset the D.I. and possibly not get anything to use in the next edition of the paper.

While the reporter was getting used to the idea, he was not getting any more information the police car was pulling away from the roadside and heading back to Lynn. Unfortunately, Ray also knew that the newspaper would get something in print, just by speaking to locals who would give them details of any gossip that would soon spread around about the recent events.

Ray was happy that the scene at the village was in good hands with Sheila and Tim there. He knew his first job back at the station would be to see Adam and bring him up to date with things. As he walked through the C.I.D. room 2 of the D.C's from the team were busy getting a corner of the room ready for all the paraphernalia that would be needed as an incident room. Ray knew he could leave them to carry on so made his way to the Superintendent's office. The secretary was at her desk busy with typing; but as the door opened, she glanced up and said,

'He is expecting you and has been for the last hour.'

'I am sure he will wish I wasn't here now once I speak to him.'

Adam may have been expecting Ray but it didn't stop him from finishing straightening up the papers on his desk, before he made any attempt to speak.

'How were your days off? Also, what has happened that took you away so quickly?'

Adam managed to make the 2nd question sound as though Ray had found an excuse not to have been and seen him sooner.

'The days off were fine, thank you. As to my reason for chasing off. We have a nasty death to deal with; a former D.I.

Steve Edwards who lived out at Terrington St Clement was discovered by the postman this morning.'

'He had retired by the time I arrived here, but he was a good officer by all accounts.'

'Yes, Sir, he was. Steve was my D.I. when I first joined C.I.D here at Lynn.'

'What are the initial thoughts about it all?'

'It is extremely early days yet, hopefully, we will know more after the post mortem. At the moment Sheila and Tim are at the scene with the local officer, and I will want an incident room over there.'

Before Adam could speak Ray continued,

'I will keep an eye on the budget as well.'

'Do not be factitious, Ray, but you are aware of the pressures I face daily.'

Ray knew how to deal with Adam and said;

'I apologise, Sir, this just feels more personal. I will get started here and let you know more as soon as I do.'

Ray had no intention of getting into further discussions with Adam so stood up and left the room briskly.

Chapter Three

Ray left Adam smarting over the comments about the budget; Adam just wished that Ray would be more understanding of the pressures he had to deal with. Ray's mind was already elsewhere; he knew he had to concentrate on the case but couldn't stop his mind from drifting back a few days. This had been when he had received the phone call from Steve Edwards asking to meet. He started to wonder as to the bearing this could have on the case. As with a lot of police work, there would be things that even in a successful case no-one would know about.

Steve had been meaning to phone Ray for the last couple of weeks, but by following the press reports he knew how busy the team would be; also, the more he thought about things the reason for wanting to talk seemed more trivial. Steve had been retired for a good few, years and was enjoying a busy life since putting his police life behind him. This made it more unnerving when about a month previously he had got a feeling of being watched. It had been nothing he could put his finger on, just now and then as he went about his routine there was the sense that he was being watched, but never seeing anyone about. At first, it happened when he was either shopping or when he was with friends at one of the many clubs he attended; then two weeks ago he sensed something outside his house usually as evening approached. It could be seen as being complacent, that because of living in a village which still had the benefit of a constable on the beat that he felt calm about it all. He convinced himself there was no reason to bring it to anyone's attention, he also remembered how he felt when there used to be a call come through from as person who could only tell the officer they were speaking to that they thought they were being followed but with no evidence. Throughout his career which had been very successful, he had had to deal with threats from criminals like most officers did. He learnt early on that the only way to deal with this side of the job was to ignore it. There had been one occasion when the threats had become more than just verbal; a criminal who Steve had been instrumental in putting in prison for ten years; on his release, he appeared outside the police station. Steve had been on his way to speak to a witness, when Jimmy Hammer had come around the corner and punched Steve, knocking him to the ground and was just about to start kicking him when two other officers came out. The end result was that by seeking some form of revenge Jimmy Hammer ended up serving four more years in prison. Out of a thirty-year career Steve didn't feel too bad that this was the only time he had been attacked like this; due to the nature of how policing used to be he had suffered some other injuries whilst carrying out his duties. This situation had changed over the years and with better equipment and planning the number of officers suffering injuries had fallen. Once Steve retired, he saw no reason to not continue living in Terrington St Clement as he had done for the past twenty-six years. The reason he had been attracted to the house was the garden and even though it would be many years before he could enjoy it properly; he always liked the time he could spend in the garden.

During the first weeks of his retirement, he spent most daylight hours in the garden and found that having been a member of a local gardening club for many years he was now able to take a full part in the activities. It soon led to him winning medals at shows for the flowers he had grown. One of the problems faced by ex-policeman was to find something to replace the buzz that was felt through the job; winning medals that had been voted for by other gardeners went some way to satisfy this side of life for Steve. Slowly he settled into a routine and soon he felt that in a different way life was just as rewarding. Even though Steve made an effort to not bring his work home with him; his circle of friends had changed recently and also the people he socialised with were more relaxed around him; this being that in the past they always believed that a policeman was never really off duty.

The day that was to be his last, was to have been a special day for Steve. Along with other members of the village garden club they had been asked to present a special exhibition at the Sandringham flower show. Steve had been in his garden early and was organising last-minute things that would enhance the display. He was feeling relaxed and excited at the same time, the weather was lovely; stood in the garden with the sun shining on his back was a good feeling. It had been arranged that the club would meet at Sandringham but he was not surprised to hear the gate open. His thought was that it would be someone from the club who would have called in to discuss the show; several of the members had also looked to Steve to help their confidence at meeting royalty as he had been in this situation several times over the years. The surprise he felt as he looked over his shoulder was cut short as the blow to the back of his head knocked him to the ground. He didn't feel the rest of the attack as he was killed by the first blow. Within ten minutes of the gate opening, it slid quietly shut behind a person who was feeling very smug. He had heard the saying many times in his life and now he knew how satisfied it felt to him that there was a time for revenge.

Ray had always found from early in his training that ability he had that would serve him well was being able to get into the minds of a criminal, sometimes though this didn't help as the criminal involved had no real thought as to why they did something. This was to be the case this time; yes, it was for revenge but there was no great thought behind it all. This would be one of the causes for the case being very difficult for the team. Ray had returned to the C.I.D room after his meeting with Adam and found it a hive of activity as the work had started on the incident room; boards had been set up to one side and Ray admitted to himself that he found it more difficult than usual when the first pictures up on the boards were from the crime scene. He always found it hard to comprehend how one person could attack another so viciously. His phone rang it was Graham,

'Hello, Ray, I will do the post mortem at two this afternoon.'

'Thanks, Graham, I will see you there.'

'Is there any news from the scene that might help?'

'Not yet I am just about to contact Sheila and find out the latest.'

As soon as the call finished Ray rang Sheila, but as he expected there was not a lot for him to hear. The early results of the house to house had all brought the same response, that nothing untoward had been seen or heard. Sheila then added,

'John has managed to get the hall opposite the house to open up a room that can be utilised as an incident room. So, I will stay here for now and get that set up with him. Tim is going to return to Lynn, so I will see you later.'

'I am attending the P.M. this afternoon so will let you know the results. You will just need to keep an eye on things there.'

As Sheila was still getting to know the area it would be helpful for her to have John with her. Sheila was happy with the situation and had already developed a respect for Ray so appreciated it that he was happy to leave in her charge in Terrington, and she had soon seen the benefits of John being the local constable. Quickly before Tim returned, he rang Jenny;

'Hello, sweetheart I think it could be late night this evening.'

He went on to explain what had happened and Jenny was concerned; she knew that Ray liked Steve and the time he worked with him had left an impression on him.

'Are you alright?'

'I will be; it will just take some adjusting to know I am dealing with the murder of a friend.'

'I will see you when you get home; I think Mum and Dad would like to go out for a meal while they are here if we can fit it in.'

'Tell them I will do my best to get it sorted. I will see you later and I love you.'

'I know and right back at you.'

This had become her answer whenever Ray told her he loved her. He was very practical about things, but she liked the fact that he was soft and romantic about his feelings for her. He put the phone down and leaned back in his chair, since his relationship with Jenny had developed Ray found that his life had changed and there were two parts to it. He always tried to keep them separate. It did help that Jenny understood how his life was; this case was to give him a lot to think about, and it meant that the two sides of his life would merge because of his friendship with Steve.

Jenny was concerned when she came off the phone; all officers knew the risk involved with the job and the possibility of a case such as this one developing. She told her mum about the call and she knew they understood but they also hoped to see Ray while they were visiting. Her dad just accepted it as part of his work, but her mum was more concerned about their safety,

'This is the one side of your job I don't like; what if it was you who got attacked?'

'You just have to realise it doesn't happen as a matter of course Mum. Every one of us takes as many precautions as possible.'

'I know but it doesn't stop me worrying.'

Jenny was well aware that if she allowed the conversation to continue, her mum would end up as usual trying to persuade Jenny to look for another job.

'Anyway, let us make a start on getting everything else unpacked as that is the reason for your visit.'

Jenny knew when her mum started to worry about her job the best thing to do was to distract her. Because of the case breaking like it had; it was to be a big help to Jenny that her mum and dad were there.

Chapter Four

Ray looked up from his desk as Tim knocked on the door,

'From your grin, I hope you have some good news for me?'

'I'm not sure if you will think of it as good news; I think it is for me. I have just been given the details for my Sergeants exam.'

Tim had progressed well since joining the force and had proved himself a valuable member of C.I.D. and Ray knew he wanted to keep progressing.

'That is good news but you might find it hard to study much at the moment.'

'I will just fit it in around the case, but obviously, the case is more important.'

'I know that is how you will deal with things and talking of the case; I need you to get onto the computer and start looking into the life of Steve Edwards. First to see if there are any clues; as much as none of us would want to discover it we need to know if he has led as clean a life since he retired as he did during his career.'

Ray was able to use the computer for his daily routine but appreciated that the younger officers were more useful with them than him.

'Anything you feel I should be looking for in particular?'

'I think anything that stands out as being unusual. The start point might be look back at his arrests and link together any criminals he put away. It sounds obvious but has he upset anyone recently.'

Tim grimaced as he recalled his first view of the body;

'Well, he certainly upset someone looking at the state of his skull.'

'That has to be our thinking, as it certainly didn't look like a random attack. I will leave you to work on that, Sheila is staying in Terrington and I have to go and meet Graham for the P.M.'

The team that Ray had assembled over his time at Lynn all had the capability to work as a team or on their own; this was ruled by each case as they were dealing with it. Despite their many differences of opinions about budgets and the number of officers Ray felt he needed; whenever a case demanded it and because he was aware of how it looked when a case was wrapped up; Adam would support Ray in his requests for extra officers. The quickest way Ray could deal with Adam was to ring him so this was his next job and despite some huffing and puffing about it, all Ray ended the call with two more officers being attached to C.I.D. It was easier than normal because of Adam's personal feelings about a good ex-officer having been killed. Ray had asked for W.P.C Jill Addy who had impressed him while working on the case involving Margaret O'Connor. Jill came into the room along with a new P.C who had just arrived at Lynn after his training. P.C James Peters had been at the station two weeks and already he was impressing his superiors.

'Good afternoon you two; Jill you can come with me to the P.M; James, if you go and see Tim Jarvis, he will give you some work to be going on with.'

Jill had attended her first-ever P.M. with Ray and despite having to force herself to stay in the room she had coped with it. They left the office and on the way to the hospital Ray gave her all the details of the case so far. Ray parked the car and they walked into the corridor that led to the mortuary. It struck Jill as always how it felt that the corridor and rooms of it were separated from the hospital even though accesses to the main buildings were easy enough. The area just had a different smell and feel about its rooms. The first person they met as usual was the technician Dennis who assisted Graham; Jill couldn't help but smile as she recalled her first meeting with him. He was such a surprise to her and since then her way to describe him to people in the green gown he wore was as the green giant used in food advertising. Dennis smiled as he spoke,

'Hello to you both; how are you then?'

She knew it was a necessary way of dealing with his work but Jill couldn't understand how he always sounded so cheerful. Ray answered,

'We are both fine, and hopefully, we will feel even better if Graham can give us some positive news after the P.M.'

'I am sure he will try his best if I can't interest you in some lunch first; Graham is waiting for you.'

Dennis smiled knowing full well neither of them would feel like eating at the moment. They followed Dennis through the swing doors into the room that was Graham's domain. Jill was surprised again by how bright the room was, she knew Graham had to see things clearly but was amazed by the number of lights that were on and the heat they gave out. Graham along with Dennis had carefully cleaned the body up; he was stood by the table ready to make a start. As he worked, he gave an account of what he was discovering, this account was recorded and would then be typed up.

'I have cleaned the wounds up and there was nothing in them to help you I'm afraid, the wounds didn't have a lot of soil in them, but it is obvious he died where he was found. You will be relieved to know it was easy to ascertain cause of death so I won't need to perform a full P.M. he died from a blow to the head.'

'What just one?'

'Let me finish Ray, he most definitely died immediately; but there were several more blows landed in a small area. It is as though the attack was particularly vicious but unnecessary as he was already dead, the extra blows are the reason he was in such a mess.'

'So, what was he hit with?'

'This is the bit you won't like; due to the mess I can only tell you he was attacked with the proverbial blunt instrument.'

'That is a great help.'

Ray couldn't keep the sarcasm out of his voice, even though he knew Graham was only telling them the facts as he found them.

'I might be able to work out later how many times he was struck but I am not promising anything. I can tell you that whatever he was hit with will have blood and bits on it, but was clean when used as there is no unusual objects in the wounds. The only other piece of information I can give you at present, is he was hit from behind and fell forward to land where the postman found him.'

While they were talking; Dennis completed his task of taking photos of the injuries.

Ray knew that at the moment they were not going to find out anymore and though it was frustrating he respected Graham was doing all he could. Graham then asked a question that in all the early aspects of the case had not been thought about,

'Did Steve have any family?'

'Not close family he never married. There was a sister who lived in Leeds. I'll get Tim to have a look into it.'

'I will get the results of the P.M. typed up and sent over to you.'

'Thanks Graham; speak later.'

Ray and Jill left the mortuary, not being any further forward than before the visit. His next hope was that the concentrated house to house would yield something.

While Ray had been at the hospital; Sheila had been admiring how much respect the local people had for John. Firstly, she was amazed by how many people had come up to them outside the house to ask for details of what had happened. Then within an hour of organising the incident room, there had been a total of 100 people in the hall to give them pieces of information; which would need sifting through. Some of the older residents were just shocked to have heard what had happened. Slowly as the day wore on there were small snippets of information that was the start of a picture building up. Two problems did have to be overcome first; they were interlinked problems. These were because it was a village it was assumed that everyone knew each other; a problem was caused by the fact that Terrington St Clement was a large village so there was the opportunity for a certain amount of anonymity. It did come to light from a few of the people who came forward that a stranger had been noticed in the area surrounding the home of Steve Edwards. Unfortunately, the reports so far were sketchy; it followed a pattern that the police were used to; a person of medium build and wearing dark clothes had been seen around. The question Sheila always asked witnesses who gave this type of information was how did they know it was a stranger; even in the short time she had been in the village today, she had spotted several people of medium build, wearing dark clothing.

As Sheila was getting ready to head back to Lynn; she received some news that cheered her up and she hoped Ray would find it pleasing. A P.C. who had been helping check the house overcame into the hall and said:

'We have found in a filing cabinet in the study, full of all of the notebooks from the victim's career.'

Sheila was about to point out that they knew the name of the victim, but looking at the young P.C. she didn't see it would help. She was aware there would be computer records from the tail end of Steve's career, but all his early work would be recorded in his notebooks.

'I want you to arrange a van and get anything relevant to the D.I.'s career over to Lynn. Then it can be gone through.'

'Yes ok, we will get it over there this evening.'

Sheila decided to ring Ray then make her way back. Ray took the news in and as it was early in the investigation; he knew it could be good news at least it would give the team something to start work on.

'I will wait here for you, and then hand over to Dave Hulme before heading home.'

Once the call was over Ray was about to go and see if Dave Hulme was already in the station when he looked up and saw his smiling face at the door,

'Interesting start back at work for you, Ray.'

'You could say that; I take it you have heard who has been killed then.'

'Yes, I got a call earlier and as well as being downright disgusting it is also a great shame. Steve Edwards was a good copper and he was always really helpful to all the young officers that started here.'

Ray brought Dave up to date with the events of the past nine hours. Ray already knew what the plan would be for the next shift to do. He just found it easier to go home once he had told Dave what was going to happen, also if there was anything they really needed to look out for.

'I'll get a couple of the team onto making a start going through all the old notebooks and we will see if we can piece anything together.'

The feeling that Ray liked about the station having a constant team in place was always helped for him in that he handed over to a regular D.I. for the late shift. Dave was a single man and he had never objected to doing a night shift or any other shift no-one else wanted. He had settled easily into life as a young P.C. and enjoyed the different feel that the late shifts had about them. As with most things in life if someone was willing to volunteer for something it soon became expected. The other reason Dave didn't mind was he was one of the people who could sleep anywhere and at any time; so his sleep patterns were the same as someone working a day shift. Ray leant back in his chair as Sheila came into the office.

'The van with all the paperwork will be here soon.'

'Right thanks Sheila; you get off home and be here for a briefing at 8 in the morning.'

'You need to get yourself off home as well Ray; I am sure Jenny is waiting patiently for you.'

Ray smiled and nearly pointed out to Sheila that it was the first time she had used his name, but didn't want to make her feel uncomfortable so let it pass.

'She will be glad to see me home at a reasonable time, but I just need to go and see Adam first.'

'There is no point; he passed me on my way in. He was looking extra smart, and the buttons on his jacket had that extra sparkle to them so I presume he has a special function to attend.'

'That is one small relief then. I will see you both tomorrow.'

Ray sat in his car for a minute and thought fondly of his memories of Steve Edwards and then he thought ahead to the journey home. Slowly he felt the smile break across his face as he knew Jenny would be waiting for him.

Chapter Five

Before he left the car park; being aware that cameras were everywhere when you didn't think about it and not wanting to be caught on film while on the phone. He rang Jenny to tell her he was just leaving. Jenny couldn't help but sound pleased as it meant Ray would be home earlier than expected.

'That is good news, Mum and Dad would like to take us out to dinner, this evening.'

'That would be nice; we could go to the Raj as we haven't been there for some time.'

The Raj was an Indian restaurant that was now local to them, but earlier in their relationship it had been a place they could visit together as no-one in the area knew them. The journey home was certainly a different experience for Ray and in contrast to the early morning trip; it was busier and within moments of leaving the car park he found himself in a slow-moving queue of traffic heading towards Southgate's roundabout. The road systems in and around the towns of Norfolk had long been a point of conversations, but nothing much ever seemed to change. Ray knew of all the moans that went on, but he did feel to a point it was part of the attraction of the area. After 15 minutes of not moving, he started to fail to see this side of things; then as was often the case for no obvious reason the traffic moved again and kept flowing freely for the rest of his journey home. As there was the feeling of comfort when they returned from dancing, it now felt good to be coming home from work and knowing that Jenny was waiting. Ray went in and said hello to everyone, it was nice that he felt Anne and David were welcoming towards him. He knew that Anne worried about Jenny in her work and now he was part of her life; it became a different worry. Like all officers, Ray put thoughts of his own safety to the back of his mind. Ray smiled as he asked Anne,

'Did you bring Charlie with you?'

Charlie was the family dog who had taken an instant liking to Ray the first time he had visited with Jenny.

'No, not this time, but we will do in the future, the house is lovely and the garden is a good size.'

David was next to speak,

'I don't know about anyone else; I am getting hungry shall we go and eat?'

'That sounds like a good idea; I am ready when you are.'

The mention of eating relaxed everyone and they went out looking forward to a nice evening. The people at the restaurant were very happy to see Jenny and Ray, the meal as always was very good and Ray thought to himself how well he had settled into this phase of his life. While they were eating and chatting, he found that he had switched off from work; something he had not found very easy in the past. The other reason he felt relaxed was knowing that once the meal was over, they were only 10 minutes from home and he was going home with Jenny whereas previous visits to the Raj had finished with them going home separately. Anne and David had booked into a local hotel as they didn't know how organised the house would be. They did all go back to the house and said goodbye, with Jenny telling her parents she would see them in the morning. As Ray was settling down, he saw the light was flashing on the answer machine; he listened to the message, it was from Dave Hulme. The first words of the message were Dave explaining that Ray didn't need to act on anything but he wanted Ray to know the latest before the morning. The officers who had been going through the notebooks from the house had made a discovery that could be a breakthrough. Ray didn't listen to the rest of the message before he dialled Dave's phone.

'I said you didn't need to do anything.'

'Just tell me what you have got.'

As Dave explained; Ray realised that it could wait until the morning but he was glad Dave had rung. It transpired that in with his official notes, Steve had also made personal notes. This was something that didn't happen on computers. One of the people Steve had used as an informer in his early career had got into some trouble and even though Steve had tried his best for the person it had ended with a prison sentence. This was part of the job that Ray was pleased had changed officers didn't use informers in the same way as they used to; it had led to trouble when people who were normally small-time criminals started passing information across, then would get greedy with their demands for reimbursement. The usual threats made from the dock to many officers had been ringing in Steve's ears as the man was led away to start his sentence. Ray ended the conversation by asking Dave to get someone to look in more detail at this information.

'I will see you in the morning.'

As he put the phone down Jenny asked;

'Have you got to go into work?'

'No, Dave has things in hand, and also it is not as easy now. That is something else I need to get used to; there is the journey and work is not just around the corner.'

'As long as you don't mind, that is the important thing.'

'I am getting used to it all. Also, the fact of how happy I am makes up for it.'

They got ready to go to bed.

The criminal that Steve was referring to in his notes and whose name was not mentioned at first was Jimmy Hammer. The sentence he received was minimal due in part to Steve putting in a good word, even though this was not appreciated by Jimmy. The time in prison was to prove a turning point in the life of Jimmy but not from a good point. As so often happened when a person went into prison for the first time and were easily led, instead of the possibility of rehabilitation it went the opposite way.

Jimmy Hammer was not the sharpest tool in the box, but aside from the threats he made to Steve Edwards; he knew it was his own fault though he was adjusting to prison life. Jimmy was not the stereo-typical criminal; he was well built and very powerful; at the same time, he was always well dressed. He had always admired good clothes and when he started passing information to Steve and got paid for it, he put the money towards looking good. He found that being well-turned out-earned him respect, after the initial response from fellow prisoners about him being a pretty boy because of his clothes; he soon settled into a routine and as the others saw his capabilities in the gym a healthy respect was built up towards him. The one obvious piece of information Jimmy had been keen to keep to himself was his career as a police informer. The prison sentence had been due to his part in a robbery with two others. They had held up a security van delivering to a petrol station, the amount stolen was very small, the thing that changed the crime was one of the others had attacked a guard with a baseball bat. After a lengthy enquiry Jimmy was the only one arrested, during the following interviews he refused to name the others. As Jimmy told his story of crime to the others with some embellishments, he soon had others hanging on his every word; he was soon enjoying his new found fame. Three weeks after entering prison he was in the mind set to be a serial criminal for years to come.

The main reason that a life of crime appealed to Jimmy was that the financial rewards were greater than the money he got from Steve; even though this amount was more than he was used to having. In many areas there were always discussions as to why a person turned to crime; it usually revolved around a bad upbringing or other such examples. In the case of Jimmy some of this could be applied, though his early childhood was reasonably happy when he became a teenager, things changed quite dramatically. His younger sister who his mum doted on was killed in an accident while riding her bike. His mum never got over this and with little or no support from his dad she turned to alcohol as a way of dealing with things. As a young child Jimmy took less notice of the home situation, then as he got older, he realised that he had never known his dad to work. After the first few times of asking if he could have computer games like his friends and being told no; he knew the only way of getting things was down to him. Because he had always been polite it was not a problem to get neighbours to pay him for doing odd jobs.

Then when he was 15; it could be said that he got in with a bad crowd. But people can be drawn together because of circumstances and this was what had happened. A group of boys at school that Jimmy had spoken to and hung around with on occasions were talking about the latest computer game they knew was out. One of them looked at Jimmy and said.

'How do you fancy a copy of that Jimmy?'

'No point really, I haven't got a player for it,'

One of the others laughed.

'That is not a problem my brother can get you one cheap.'

'Yes, then how do I afford the game?'

'You don't have to. You have seen the security guard at the games shop, he couldn't catch a cold.'

This brought raucous laughter from the others. Slowly Jimmy realised what was being suggested. Deciding that he would really like the game he said.

'Ok then what do we do?'

Within two hours Jimmy had become a criminal, picking the game up and running out of the shop had been easy. Outrunning the guard had proved even easier. Because of the speed of things happening; they were soon at the house of one of the others playing the game on their console. He knew what he had done was wrong but he had got such a rush of adrenalin that this thought was pushed to the back of his mind. In a matter of weeks, Jimmy was getting more daring in his shoplifting to the point where some of the others were shocked by his behaviour. Then one afternoon after school purely by chance Jimmy had his first encounter with Steve Edwards. A group of the friends was taking the chance to get another new game; none of them was aware that there was a new security guard on duty. As Jimmy ran out of the shop the guard was out of the office and after him like a sprinter. He caught Jimmy within 400 meters of the shop. The others had all run off in different directions. If the guard had just taken Jimmy back to the store and called the police; things may have turned out differently. Instead, because Jimmy was not at all bothered by being caught and then swore at the man; the guard reacted totally wrong and went to hit out at Jimmy. He raised his arm just as Steve Edwards was walking past. Steve grabbed the man's arm:

'I am sure there is no need for that.'

As Steve had hold of the guard's arm, Jimmy saw his chance to get away and darted to his left. Steve put out his right arm and in an authoritative voice said:

'That will not do anyone any good.'

Jimmy was sensible enough to know how far to go. Suddenly he saw the situation could be turned to his advantage. He didn't see it was necessary to cry but in a very quiet voice he said,

'He was going to hit me and I said I was sorry.'

Steve looked at the guard.

'You are not going to believe that are you?'

'I just know what I saw and you were going to hit him.'

'I know I shouldn't have done that, but him and his mates have been stealing from the shop for weeks.'

Steve showed the man his warrant card:

'Right well I will take over from here; someone from the station will contact you at the shop for a statement.'

He looked at Jimmy who had been standing quietly due to Steve still having hold of him by the shoulder. Jimmy had also realised he was in trouble so decided being quiet was a good course of action.

'You can come with me young man and we will see how we are going to deal with things.'

Once back at the station Steve asked for the names of the others that had been in the shop as the guard had mentioned. Jimmy was adamant that he had been alone. During the afternoon at the station, Steve got an address and phone number for Jimmy's parents and the custody officer rang to inform them of what had happened. He first spoke to the mother who was obviously drunk; then the father showed little interest in the situation. Steve knew that social services would possibly need to get involved, but he was keen to avoid this happening if he could. As he was taking Jimmy to the canteen to get a drink; one of the new P.Cs was just coming in for his rest period. He spoke to Steve:

'I know that lad; his sister died in an accident a couple of years ago. Having met the family, I'm surprised we have not seen him in here sooner.'

After hearing this and talking things through with his superiors it was decided to let Jimmy away with a caution, along with the warning to keep out of further trouble. The only problem with this was Jimmy was left with the impression he could now get away with certain things because of his family history. Over the next two years, Steve crossed paths on a regular basis with Jimmy, always being involved in petty crime and always insisting he was on his own.

Then one day he knew he was in more bother than usual. Steve saw the signs so made Jimmy an offer that if he was to help catch the others, Steve would put in a good word for him.

Jimmy may have been slow on certain things but he was not silly.

'If I give you names, what is it worth?'

At first Steve told him just being dealt with less seriously should be enough, but Steve also knew how helpful it was having people on the streets getting information.

'I think we can reach an agreement of sorts.'

This agreement lasted for some time until Jimmy got greedy and ended up doing his first serious time in jail.

Unknown to Ray and his team at present was how these events had led up to today and also what was going to happen over the next 72 hours.

Ray and Jenny went to bed he knew again he was wrapped up in a case as he tried to get to sleep, but with the latest information running through his head. As he cuddled up to Jenny, he slowly relaxed and the next thing he was aware of was the silence being disturbed by the alarm clock.

Chapter Six

After a slower journey into work due to a minor accident. Ray stood at the front of the room and waited as all of those present fell silent. The briefing would follow the pattern of many that had taken place over the years; though this one had an extra solemn feel to it. Ray could sense how the team were feeling and knew he would have to work hard to get them on track and keep on top of the case.

'Right morning everyone. You would have heard of what was discovered last night in the belongings from Steve Edwards' house.'

Surprisingly a couple of the team hadn't caught up with the news and Ray gave the room a few minutes for each of them to hear about the notebooks. He allowed the chatter to carry on for a few minutes; then by a simple cough he had the attention of the room again.

'There are officers who are going to have a day inside going through those notebooks. I want people out on the street; looking for this Jimmy Hammer. Depending on when his last prison stint was and his release date we should get some information that way.'

Sheila spoke next:

'If we start in Lynn; it would be easier for someone to keep a low profile in the town rather than out in a village.'

'Good point Sheila; now I know feelings will be running high during this investigation. Just remember to keep calm as you are going about your job.'

Ray looked around the room and could see and sense the feeling hanging over everyone.

'Now all of you are good at your job; you all know we are heading towards the first crucial point in the case, as we approach 24 hours since the discovery of the body. The questions may be up on this board somewhere, but the answers we need are out there and the people you need to speak too as well. Get out and bring the answers back here so we can piece it all together.'

Ray wound up the briefing by allocating the workload for all of the team for that day; this was easy enough as they all had a good idea of what was expected from each of them. All of them moved around the room either to sit at a desk or to pick up necessary items and make their way out to the streets. Sheila waited until they were all occupied then spoke to Ray;

'I think I will make my way over to Terrington first and see how things are progressing.'

'Good idea, John is most probably already there. I will go and see Adam; then I need to look at the appropriate notebooks and see what we can make of them.'

As usual, Adam started the conversation along the lines he frequently did during an enquiry:

'Any breakthrough yet Ray?'

As Ray answered he saw the disappointment briefly flash across Adam's face,

'Nothing concrete so far, though there are some lines of enquiry we are following up.'

'Surely the obvious one is he was a retired officer and it was someone with a grudge.'

Ray couldn't help but feel he was being told his job, or that Adam was just making the point that he was the superior officer.

'We are looking at that angle, Sir; we should know more by the end of the day.'

It was as though Ray had told him that they were close to wrapping up the case as Adam smiled.

'Well, that would be good. We gave the press a statement yesterday, but I will wait and hold a press conference this afternoon by which time you can give me more details.'

Ray walked out of the room feeling exasperated at how Adam reacted and knowing that there could possibly be little to add by the afternoon. No one was aware that by later that day there would be some major news but none of it would be good.

When Sheila arrived at Terrington she was taken aback, by the fact that even though it was still early in the morning; already there was a small gathering of people at the village hall to pass over snippets of information to the team. John had organised the room so that the main details were on a board at the far end of the hall; not visible to people entering the room. As anyone entered, they were met by two constables behind a desk; who proficiently went through the information they had and then decided if it needed passing further along the chain of command immediately or could wait to be looked at later in the day as an overview of the case would take place each evening.

'John, I think I will take a walk around the village and get used to the area; if you have it all under control here.'

'That is fine; I will call you if anything important turns up.'

Sheila went out of the hall; and looked across at the house opposite with the blue and white police tape fluttering in the breeze around the front door. There was still a police presence at the house even though the numbers were less than yesterday. Some of the residents had laid floral arrangements at the gate. She couldn't help but think that this was a fairly recent phenomenon that now happened at sites of tragedy. Cynically her thought was at least florists made money from these tragedies. She acknowledged the constable stood by the doorway and then walked away from the house towards the church tower that she could see reaching up to the skyline. When she got to the church she was impressed and taken aback by the size of the church being in a village. As she was to discover on this walk and over the coming days the word village was not how she would have described Terrington St Clement. Sheila was not religious but felt drawn to go in and view the church. As she walked through the archway and along the path to the side of the church, she spotted a man who when he turned towards her the flash of white at his neck revealed him to be the vicar.

'Morning, Sir.'

'Good morning, am I right to presume you are with the police?'

'Is it that obvious?'

'Only in that I do not recognise you as a villager, though I would expect some visitors once the news spreads about the body, I thought it was a bit soon for that.'

'I am D.S. Sheila Carr and you are?'

'Reverend John Tidy, I have been the vicar here for 12 years.'

'So, you know all the locals and spotted me as an outsider.'

'I know the majority; we are lucky here that the number of church goers is still good. And if I don't know people as parishioners, I see them around during my day-to-day routines.'

Sheila was about to move on as she didn't want to spend too long away from the investigation, when the next words from John made her pause.

'Have you spoken to Jimmy Hammer yet?'

Not wanting to give too much away and having learnt through her career that it helped to let people speak of their own accord; Sheila just looked at the vicar:

'As of yet no; it is a name that has been mentioned to us. So do you think he is someone we need to talk to?'

'I would have thought so, I know from conversations with Steve Edwards that if he had not intervened over the years then Jimmy would have spent more time in prison then he has already done.'

'Have you seen this person around the village recently?'

Sheila was now switched on to interview mode and wanted to get as much information as possible to take back with her.

'I have not seen him in a while; Steve used to spend time talking to Jimmy normally sat in the churchyard, just behind where you are standing in fact.'

Sheila looked round at three benches in a pattern around a piece of ground covered in plaques. She realised that even though it was a public place; at certain times it would be quite private.

'I admit that it was not recently and always assumed that it was to do with the work Steve did, but I have no more details than that.'

Sheila wanted to see more of the village but also knew that Ray would want to hear this news. She left the vicar saying how much she admired the church, and also, they may want to speak to him again. He was happy for the police to contact him if needed and also said if he could help with any background knowledge he would do.

As she left the church yard, she rang Ray, he was pleased to hear the news:

'That is another link between the two of them, I will let everyone know it is now a priority we trace Jimmy Hammer.'

Sheila knew there was not a lot to be achieved by her returning immediately to Lynn and decided it would benefit her more to carry on with get used to the surroundings. The hope she had was that she may meet other people who could give her more information. From the church and due to John having given her brief details of the village, she knew to the left were the two village schools and the post office. She turned right and made her way along and saw that one of the two pubs in the village was just opening. She decided to introduce herself so made her way into the bar. Due to it only just opening there was no one in yet, behind the bar a man and woman were getting things ready; she introduced herself and asked if either of them knew of Jimmy. The response was a grunt from the man and raised eyebrows from the woman; knowing how some landlords felt towards authority she decided not to push the issue immediately. The so far one-sided conversation ended with her telling them that some officers may be along later to talk to people. She knew that the majority of the customers may have already been to the village hall, there was just the chance that by an officer visiting the pub someone who might not have been happy about going to talk to the police would have some information to pass on. They may be more willing to do this in a relaxed atmosphere. This was a fact of modern life that happened in every town. Saying goodbye, she made her way further up the street; taking the next turning right, knowing this would take her in a circle back to the hall. Having now got it in mind to call in at the 2nd pub in the village she was just taking in the surroundings as she walked. Not really seeing any need to call into shops as she knew this was work that was being done by the uniformed officers working the case. As she made her way past an impressive looking building; which John had told her used to be the Crown Court building. It amazed her that a village would have a Crown Court but even now the aura of the building took her breath away; and she was able to imagine what it would have once been like. She was about to continue on her way when a lady called across the street to her;

'Excuse me, you are with the police, aren't you?'

'That is right. I am D.S. Sheila Carr.'

The lady was now forcefully walking across the road and seemingly brushed aside the reply as she carried on talking;

'I wanted to know if you had made any effort to speak to Jimmy Hammer.'

Sheila was astounded that twice in 15 minutes this name had been mentioned to her.

'We are tracking him down as part of our enquiries; but if you have any information that could help?'

The lady was Brenda Roebuck; her family had lived in the village many years and Brenda had been born in the village. She had married a local farmer; they enjoyed a comfortable life; Brenda liked people to think well of her and though she acted posh this was more in hope than reality. While she was talking to Sheila she made a point of always moving her hands so that the person she was talking to was always watching her as much as listening to her. After a lengthy piece of conversation all one sided by Brenda, she got to the information that Sheila took an interest in.

'At school and in their teenage years my boy Jeff was friends with Jimmy. I always felt he was a bad influence on Jeff; they always seemed to spend their time with a gang of boys despite my efforts to give Jeff the best.'

'So would Jeff possibly know where Jimmy is now?'

'I do not think so; I made a point of telling Jeff to have nothing to do with him, when Jimmy first went to prison.'

She said the word prison as though she had detected a bad smell in the air.

'Well, if I could just talk to him, he may be able to help us.'

For a moment Brenda was the quietest she had been since she first called out to Sheila. Slowly she gathered herself and spoke again:

'Jeff left home two years ago and I do not know where he went.'

'Did you report it at the time?'

'What was there to report he was an adult and he made his feelings towards myself and his father plain. Then he left the house telling us not to try and contact him.'

'Did you try to find out where he was?'

Mrs Roebuck was indignant at this question:

'Well of course we did; in the end, even I had to accept that Jeff had made his decision so I had to live with it.'

'Thank you for the chat, Mrs Roebuck and we will follow it up; if we find anything out that may be of help to you, I will let you know.'

As she left Brenda and made her way back round to the village hall, Sheila was busy trying to sort through the information she now had and how it could help them. By the sounds of things, home life had not been easy for Jeff; despite what his mum said. This could mean that Jeff may have more contact with Jimmy than was known about. As she approached the hall, she was surprised to see Ray's car parked by the gate, at least she wouldn't need to ring him to bring him up to date. When Sheila went in, she said:

'I didn't expect to see you here, Sir.'

'It is alright; I am not checking up on you. I just feel better knowing Adam has to make a phone call if he wants to talk to me.'

This brought smiles to all those who heard the comment as they knew of the strained relations that were between Ray and Adam. As she relayed her conversations with the vicar and then with Brenda; she wasn't surprised when John said;

'I know all about Jeff Roebuck, but I must admit I didn't think he was a particular friend of Jimmy's. He was a bit of a tearaway but never in major trouble. Mind you if you have met his mum, you can understand why he left home.'

Sheila smiled;

'I did think that could be a reason behind him leaving; it could help us if we can find him to talk to. If as his mum told me they were in this gang of youths, they may have kept in touch.'

Ray intervened;

'We need to find Jimmy first; but get a report issued to everyone, that we are also looking for Jeff Roebuck as well.'

None of them knew that they would find Jeff before the day was finished.

Chapter Seven

As Ray and the rest of the team were getting ready to head back to Lynn; and the evening briefing of the day's work. Joe Bark was greeting the vicar at the church and preparing to meet the bell ringers who would arrive soon for the evening's practice. The vicar told him about his conversation with Sheila earlier in the day, and Joe told him that it would be no surprise if Jeff was involved somewhere along the line.

'I always thought he was a wrong sort; despite what his mum told everyone.'

'We must not judge until we know everything.'

Joe already had made his mind up about things, but left it unsaid, he needed to get ready for the evening. There were eight regular bell ringers and they met every Monday evening. The sound of their practice filled the air each week and was looked upon as part of the village. Joe was always first to arrive and he would go into the ringing room and drop all the bell ropes into place and have things ready for the others. Tonight was their last practice before they would ring the bells as part of the church flower festival the following weekend. The others arrived and after a few minutes talking they took their places; to get the right effect the bells were rung in a certain order and each bell was a different size. There were six smaller bells and one large main bell. The first four ropes were pulled into place, the first pull on a rope swung the bell into place then as it was slowly released the bell moved back and the clanger inside rang the note. Slowly the four bells started to ring in a round then the fifth came into place the bell ringer pulled the rope and knew immediately something was not right. The rope was pulled down so far then jammed. The others all looked over with the same thought of what was wrong Ted was one of the most experienced ringers so obviously knew it didn't feel right. Before Joe could go up the next flight of stairs to see what was wrong, the others had to allow their bells to swing back to a resting position. Slowly the bells fell silent and Joe went through the small doorway that would take him up to the bells. Within six steps and at the first corner he was brought to a stop. Lying across the stairs at a twisted angle was a body. After the shock of body; Joe was even more stunned to see it was someone he knew. It appeared that Jeff Roebuck was closer to home than his mum knew about. The next few moments were more unusual after a discovery of a body, Joe didn't scream in fact he uttered no sound. Partly this was due to him having served as an ambulance man for many years, and he had dealt with all types of calls from hospital call outs to attending many road accidents. He returned through the door much quicker than the others had expected; one of them asked:

'That was sharp Joe what was wrong?'

'I don't know yet, there is a body on the stairs. Can someone ring the police?'

Another member spoke up;

'Shall we see if we can get them down of the stairs?'

Joe replied,

'No, I can tell you they are dead and the police would prefer it if we leave everything as it is. We should all go and wait downstairs for now.'

So far, they still had no idea what had stopped the bell ringing.

The 999 call had been put through to Ray as he was finishing up the briefing. As soon as the caller had said about a body at Terrington St Clement it was passed over to him. No one made any comment about not being able to finish work; Ray gave them five minutes to let families know they would be home late then called the room to order. This phone call home was important as Ray remembered early in his career working a case late and not having a chance to let Mary know; she had heard on the news about an incident locally and had worried until he got home. He had decided that once in a position of leadership that his team should always let families know about unexpected happenings. Very quickly the team were poised and ready to move. Tim Jarvis had already spoken to Graham Keys and Lisa Hall so the doctor and the forensics team would meet them at the church. Due to nature of the 999 call; the air around the station was soon filled with the noise of sirens; while blue lights flashed on to everywhere surrounding the cars. The day was turning to dusk so the lights cast their rapid glow further, this did mean that traffic seemingly moved out of the way easily. Soon the convoy of cars were out onto the A17 and the journey to the scene ended less than 10 minutes after it started. Graham and Lisa despite starting out sooner had slower journeys and pulled into the car park to find police vehicles parked at random angles in front of the church, with the light bars on the roofs still flashing and creating a light show on the houses opposite. Already there was a P.C. standing by the gate with a clipboard and he would record names and times for everyone who now entered or left the scene. Lisa found it poignant that the gate was still adorned with flowers from a recent wedding. Her experience was such that she was able to switch off from the fact, that somewhere that recently was a celebration of events was now full of sadness; she had soon learnt that murderers didn't think of such things. Graham had arrived on his own knowing that his visit would be the quickest as his main work would be carried out at the mortuary with the post mortem. He was required at the scene for a legal point of view that as silly as it seemed they had to have a doctor confirm death. He would always help if he could by giving a summary of his first thoughts surrounding the situation, of all the people he worked with he liked Ray in that he would not push for answers immediately as much as he might like to. On the other hand, Lisa had the majority of her team with her as their work would revolve around the scene of the crime. As they walked towards the church, they discussed what either of them knew about this latest crime, as it was the details both had were similar and not a great deal. The calls they had received from Tim had just told them there had been a body discovered in the church at Terrington, it sounded so ironic of a body in a church that it could be the start of a bad joke. As in the past, this sense of humour helped people through the very black moments of their work. Graham and Lisa met up with Ray and Sheila at the doorway of the church and went inside; at first, neither of them could grasp how many people were standing around in the pews at the back of the church.

'Evening Ray are these witnesses or potential suspects?'

'Neither I don't think, they are the bell ringers who were here for their practice. One of them found the body.'

Graham scanned the group:

'Any useful early information from anyone?'

'I don't think we will get much as they were only here for 15 minutes when they phoned us.'

At this point, Tim came to join them with a man standing behind him.

'Sir; this is Joe Bark he is the head bell ringer and it was himself who discovered the body.'

'Thanks, Tim do we know the circumstances behind the discovery?'

'Only that the bell ringers had started the practice, when one of the bells didn't ring. Joe went to investigate and discovered the body on the stairs.'

'Right, we will need a full statement from you Sir; first I would like you to show us up to the bell tower. Tim can you get details from all the others; then they can go home. And get someone to contact the vicar.'

Joe with Ray, Sheila and Graham following made their way to the bell tower. Lisa and her team were working on the edge of the church looking for anything that could suggest how the body had got there. Ray could remember a few years previously visiting the church on an open day and knew there was a room first where the bell ringers stood then there was a set of narrow steps up to the bells. Joe repeated the details of his discovery as they reached this first room.

'Did you recognise the body at all?'

'Not at first, I initially checked for a pulse; it is the first time we have had someone in here, but the church itself does get the odd homeless person sneak in for a night. I did then realise it was Jeff Roebuck.'

'Fine if you can show the doctor where the body is please; then I don't think we will need to bother you anymore so you can go home.'

'Ok, but I would like to check and see what it is that has stopped the bell from working.'

'Just let us check things first, and then it should be ok for you to check.'

Joe showed Graham where the body was; Graham had already decided on the first staircase that once he confirmed death. He would get the body moved as he could not work in such a confined space. This decision was even easier to make as he saw the body crammed into the stairwell up to the bells. He called down to Ray:

'He has been dead approximately 24–48 hours I will tell you more after the P.M. You can get the guys to take the body away and before you ask there is no obvious cause of death that I can see.'

'Thanks for that, Graham.'

Ray moved to one side to allow the men through to the stairwell; he started to think how could this be connected to the murder of Steve Edwards if at all. It would be far-fetched but it could also just be a coincidence. His thoughts were interrupted by a shout from Graham:

'Ray, you need to see this.'

He squeezed up the stairs past the men from the mortuary:

'I have now found the cause of death; he has been stabbed in the neck. Then the body was moved here as there is no sign of blood.'

Next Graham held up the left arm of the victim, Ray could see the hand was missing. He spoke quietly to Graham.

'Before you move the body, I want to get Joe Bark downstairs out of the way.'

Graham nodded then after a few minutes heard Joe say:

'But I want to find out what has stopped the bell working.'

'I know you do, but there has been a development and I need my team to be able to go through, this area first. As it now is being treated as a crime scene.'

Ray was already thinking he knew exactly what was stopping the bell from ringing. He got Sheila to take Joe down to the church:

'When you get down there before you go home can you show D.S. Carr the entrances to the bell tower, if I remember correctly there are two ways up here.'

'That is correct through the church like we came; or there is a doorway outside in the churchyard. That door is not used at the moment as it needs repairing.'

'I would still like you to show D.S.Carr.'

Joe went downstairs with Sheila as two men brought the body down to put it onto a stretcher. They would need to make it secure before carrying it to the van. As they went down, Graham and Ray went up further to the top of the bell tower. Joe had told him that it was the 2nd bell on the right that didn't ring. When they got into the bell room Ray leant against the wooden railing that surrounded the bells; the size of the bells was amazing and it surprised people when they saw them how they could be moved by anyone pulling the rope below. It took Ray a moment but he soon saw exactly what had stopped the bell ringing. Jammed between the bell and its frame was the left hand of the victim.

'Well, at least I will not have a problem getting his fingerprints at the P.M.'

Ray didn't answer as he knew Graham meant nothing by the comment. Graham carefully reached through the frame and removed the hand.

'This has been thought out Ray; there was no blood on the stairs and there is none here.'

'I agree and also I would say they wanted us to find the body, by stopping the bells working. If you get back and can get the P.M done; Lisa and the team can get in here to see if they can find any clues.'

They made their way down to meet with the others; Sheila stepped forward and spoke:

'Two pieces of news Sir; John recognised the body; it is Jeff Roebuck. The boy whose mother I was talking to earlier. The next piece of news is you need to come and look at the outside door. The lock is broken and I would think that is how the killer got the body in where he did.'

'I know who the victim is and I will be outside in a moment; Tim can you get back to the station and add this information to what we have already. Then look into any connections between our two victims also between Jeff and Jimmy Hammer.'

Ray then turned to John:

'Can you do the same in the incident room in the village please.'

Both men moved off to do as asked. Sheila took Ray and Lisa to investigate the damage to the doorway. His first thought when he saw the door was how out of the way it was. Sheila spoke first:

'Are we really thinking that Jeff Roebuck was killed somewhere else, then brought here and carried up the stairs.'

'It does seem far-fetched but Jeff wasn't exactly well built and if the information we have had about Jimmy is true, he is strong and works out. Lisa see what you can find out around this area, and then work on the stairs and the room where the bell ringers stand. Has anyone contacted the vicar?'

'Yes, I did, he is making his way over.'

As Sheila finished her reply, the vicar came around the corner with a W.P.C. he looked at Sheila;

'Hello again, not good news for the church.'

Ray spoke next:

'Not good news for the victim either.'

'I'm sorry I didn't mean any disrespect; I just don't expect things like this to happen here.'

Ray carried on as he was not sure how much use if any the vicar could be:

'This doorway does not look the strongest; especially if you are trying to stop people getting in.'

'We don't normally make a point of wanting to stop anyone getting into church.'

'I understand that; but surely in this day and age you have areas you prefer the public not to have access to.'

Sheila was soon aware that the conversation about security could easily overshadow the important matter at hand.

'Can I just ask; when was the last time this doorway was checked.'

'I checked all the entrances last week and it was locked then.'

Lisa called them over:

'Ray come and see this; you can see where the door has been forced.'

'Any idea what was used to force it.'

'Not really; a guess would be a crowbar or the claw end of a hammer.'

By now the light was starting to fade and Ray knew the chances of finding any clues outside was reducing.

'Lisa if you have a look at the room upstairs; I think it would be best if we seal this door up for tonight and make a fresh start in the morning.'

As much as Ray would like to continue, he was aware that there came a point when not a lot more could come forward to help an investigation. With all the team rested after a night's sleep they could all start full-on in the morning.

'What about the church for tonight?' Asked the vicar.

'We will have officers here throughout the night; we will be back in the morning. For the next day or two, I am afraid this is a crime scene.'

As much as the vicar was not happy about this, he had soon realised that Ray was in charge of things so agreed with this situation.

'Sheila if you go back to the station and as long as everything is in place there; tell the team to report back tomorrow morning at 7am. There will be a briefing; then we will get things moving.'

'What about you, Sir?'

'I will take W.P.C. Addy and go and see Mrs Roebuck. Then call Adam; after which I will make my way home and see you in the morning.'

The next task was the part of the job; that Ray had never really ever got used to. Delivering news of the death of a loved one never got any easier. There were several aspects of the job that all officers had to accept. Ray had never had a problem dealing with all the traumas he came across in his work, but he could remember clearly the first time he had accompanied another officer to pass on the news that a loved one had died. The lady who had received this news literally crumbled to the floor in front of him; he did think afterwards that it was lack of experience that meant he did not know what to do. But even after all this time he always found that he felt useless. When they arrived at the home of Mrs Roebuck his first surprise was that there was a Mr Roebuck; he didn't know why but he had formed the opinion that Jeff's mum lived alone. Once they were in the front room and within five minutes, he could see why this opinion had formed, it was obvious that Mrs Roebuck was in charge of all aspects of the home. Ray asked her to sit down then watched the colour drain from her face as he gave her the news. He was then shocked as she let out a wail and burst into tears. Fortunately, Jill was on hand to deal with the lady. His next shock was that Mr Roebuck made no attempt to comfort his wife; he just stood up and walked out of the room. The next noise they heard was the front door closing.

'Jill stay here, I will be back in a moment.'

Ray went out after Mr Roebuck; he caught up with him as he went through a gate into one of the fields he owned as part of the farm.

'Mr Roebuck, you did not seem shocked by the news just now.'

'We haven't heard from our son for two years and even before that he didn't have a lot of time for us; despite what his mum might say. You could say that I have been waiting for this news for some time.'

Ray soon realised that he was not going to get any useful answers from Mr Roebuck; so, expressed his sympathy and left him to wander around the edge of the field. When he went back into the house Mrs Roebuck had quietened her sobbing and Jill was sat on the sofa beside her.

'Do you want us to arrange for a female officer to spend the night here, or will you be alright Mrs Roebuck. I do not think we need disturb you anymore tonight.'

All Ray got in return was a nod and another wail of grief. Jill got up to join him and as they left the front room; they heard the back door open, and Mrs Roebuck say:

'Oh, it is only you.'

The grunted reply Ray recognised as her husband.

'We need to come back in the morning to see how she is, I do not think there is going to be much support from her husband.'

'If you like, Sir, I can come here and speak to her.'

'That will work well, Jill. Report to me after you have spoken to her and see if you can find out more about Jeff and his friendship with Jimmy.'

Chapter Eight

The briefing room was full of noise when Ray got in from his journey; he was running late due to there having been an accident which had caused the already busy traffic to snarl up completely. The only positive for him was it gave him some time to think about the case. He ended up moving off with the traffic feeling frustrated at the fact that now they had two bodies but were no further forward. The newspaper headline he saw when he entered the room didn't help his mood. In bold letters across the header of the local paper were the words;

Police in Hunt for Serial Killer

No one in the team classed it as a serial killer but the press had all they needed in the information they had been given by the police press officer. There had now been two bodies discovered in the same village. Ray was always aware that keeping his team focused was a big part of his job. Fortunately, the team had been together long enough that it was easy to get them to ignore the press coverage. He knew that the newer members joining the team to help with the case; would need warning about who they spoke to, he would do this separately after the briefing.

'Right newspapers away and let us move forward on this case.'

Sheila spoke next:

'The forensics team are returning to the church today. so hopefully, they will turn up something to help.'

'Good; next question did Jimmy and Jeff just happen across each other again recently or have they been in contact for longer. Tim, I want you to see what you can find out on this. See if you can find a mobile phone Jeff had use of. Also, try to find out where Jeff has been living.'

Ray turned towards the whiteboards set up in the room and studied the pictures that were starting to be assembled on it. Suddenly there was a lot of murmuring in the room and Ray turned to see Adam stood at the doorway.

'A word with everyone please Detective Inspector?'

'Certainly Sir; quiet people.'

Adam moved to the front of the room and Ray still found it hard to grasp that even though he knew how busy the team were; before he started to speak Adam appeared to make sure he was standing in the centre of the room. He then adjusted the sleeves of his jacket and touched all the buttons.

'I presume you have all seen the press reports this morning. It is not going to do anyone any good if the public are scared because of the things they are reading.'

Fortunately, only Ray heard the comment from the side of the room.

'Talk about stating the bleeding obvious.'

Adam carried on; 'The one thing to help is a quick result and to show the press; how with good police work a case is solved. I know you will all have work to do so keep going and let us see this wrapped up as quickly as we can.'

Ray had lost count of the number of times he had heard these sorts of words from Adam. He also knew it didn't do any good at all. The one benefit was it made Adam feel better and he would leave the room feeling he had given morale a boost. By doing so it earned Ray a few hours where Adam wouldn't pester him. Ray had learnt quickly when he first got promoted to D.I. that after Adam had been in the room speaking, he needed to move the team on quickly. As Adam left the room, sometimes before he was even out of the room there would be murmurs of discontent around the room along the lines of does, he knows what we have to put up with.

Ray stood at the side of the room and cleared his throat; this was enough to get everyone's attention. He would never voice his opinion to the team about Adam, despite realising that they most probably knew how he felt;

'Right, you all heard the Superintendent; get to your jobs and let us see what progress we can make.'

As the team all left to their desks or made their way out of the room Ray spoke to Sheila:

'If you keep control of things here; see what more you can find out about the connection between Steve, Jimmy and now Jeff. I will go and see how forensics are doing at the church.'

'Certainly, Sir; I feel the link between Jimmy and Jeff is important and needs exploring more. I would like to go and talk to Mrs Roebuck some more.'

'That sounds like a good idea, but tread carefully with her. As you will be aware, she is not going to be at her best also there is very little support from her husband.'

Ray knew Sheila would be fine so he left her and went to make the journey to Terrington St Clement and the church. The next conversation Ray was to have would not be the sort he wanted to have nor would he hear anything good. As he was making his way out of the station the desk sergeant called to him:

'Ray there is a phone call for you.'

He was impatient to get to the church to hear from forensics as to what they had found in daylight.

'Who is it?'

'A Detective Constable Sam Penn. He wants to talk to you about Steve Edwards.'

Ray walked to the phone in the corner of the front office and picked it up.

'D.I. Ray Keane speaking.'

'Hello, Sir, I am D.C. Sam Penn. I am now based in Colchester but I worked with Steve Edwards when I first joined the force.'

'That sounds as though it may have been a few years ago.'

'Certainly, is and it does feel like a long time ago these days. I was 18 and Steve was still a D.S when I met him.'

Ray allowed Sam the time to explain his time in the force and the fact he was approaching retirement. Then he felt he needed to get to the point of the call.

'So, what do you have to tell me then, Sam?'

'Just that I saw the news about Steve and wondered about the details surrounding his killing. He was a good officer; but when I worked with him, I did feel he went close to overstepping the line sometimes.'

This was not the sort of thing Ray wanted to hear and he would not want the press to getting this information.

'In what way as I worked with Steve and always had respect for him as a good officer.'

He couldn't keep the defensive tone out of his voice; bad mouthing a fellow officer, especially a now dead one didn't sit well with Ray.

'Don't get me wrong Sir; he was a very good officer, I just felt sometimes in dealing with information he would do what he needed to get a result. And as with a lot of officers at the time the rules didn't always get followed.'

'In what way do you think he did things wrong?'

'Only that he exerted pressure on some of his informants to say more than they knew if it ended with the result he wanted.'

Ray thought back to the notebooks that had been found at Steve's house and the information that was written in them about Jimmy Hammer.

'Sam, can you write down what you can remember about things from then; and email me so I can see if it has any bearing on our case.'

'Not a problem, Sir, and I know it is not nice to hear things like this. But I just want to say Steve was good to me and he didn't deserve this.'

'Thanks, Sam; I may need to speak to you again about this.'

Ray finished the call and decided he needed a few minutes to digest this information before driving to Terrington. He walked out of the front of the station and into the park opposite. He had always enjoyed a chance to walk in the park and used it as good thinking time. He certainly had a lot to think about. The view around the park had changed over recent years with the local authority spending a lot of money to attract more visitors and Ray had been of the opinion that the money could prove to be wasted if the park got ruined by vandalism. So far it seemed that people had respect for the facilities that had been put in and especially in good weather it got a lot of use. The view out of the park was also changing. Nelson Court for many years had been a blot on the landscape; a typical 1960's built complex of flats over the years it had become run down and a bolt hole for various villains. The previous year it had been announced that the local housing authority had decided to refurbish a lot of the flats and the surrounding area. At present the view was of a lot of scaffold around the building and also a lot of noise of building work. If people had been sceptical about the money spent on the park; there was disbelief about spending anything on the flats. Ray was of the same thought but he knew something had to be done.

As he walked around the park, he tried to digest the phone call from Sam Penn; he just could not believe that Steve was the type of policeman that Sam had been inferring he was. He realised that previously there had been a lot of officers who once in C.I.D saw it as a chance to assert pressure on people and knew they were protected by the job; he just could not believe Steve was like this. He also was aware of the pressures they all faced to get results; so, he knew that he would have to get it all investigated once he had the email from Sam.

He now felt ready to drive to the church and see if anything there could help. Ray was hoping for some good news and he got this on his arrival at the church. Lisa met him in the car park, and he could tell by her look that they had found something.

'I hope the news you have reflects your smile.'

'I certainly hope so; it could be your first piece of good luck.'

Ray had always gone along with the theory that police work was 75% good detective work and 25% good luck. Lisa held up an evidence bag and Ray found it difficult to believe that the small piece of cloth he was struggling to see in the bottom of the bag could be of any help to them.

'And this item is what exactly?'

'This is a piece of cloth from some clothing; I'm not sure which type yet.'

'Could it not be from anything?'

'Don't be a pessimist, Ray, I can tell you it does not match colour wise anything the victim was wearing; the bell ringers told me that people very rarely need to venture up those stairs.'

'So, we hope it snagged off something our criminal was wearing?'

Ray always did his best to control his emotions in front of others and didn't like to get his hopes up too quickly. He knew though that this could be a breakthrough in gathering evidence to build a case eventually.

'Right, Lisa, if you get the material back with you and do your stuff. Let me have the results as soon as you can thanks. I will speak to you later.'

His plans for the rest of the day were to catch up with John at the incident room and hear of any new information; then head back to Lynn for the evening briefing.

Chapter Nine

The evening briefing was to be a frustrating meeting as apart from the piece of material; there was no new information to help. Tim Jarvis had found out that Jimmy and Jeff had been in a gang together throughout their youth; despite the gang being in trouble several times, Jeff had never been a target for the police. It seemed that he was just happy to be thought of as a member of the gang. This was how Steve Edwards had first encountered Jimmy.

'As of yet I have not been able to trace any of the other members of the gang, but I will keep working on it.'

Ray was aware that they were all feeling as frustrated as he was.

'It has been nearly three days since the body of Steve Edwards was discovered and all of you have put a lot of hours in. I feel this case is going to take some more time yet; so, get yourselves home and rested. Be back here at 7 tomorrow morning.'

As people started to move away from their desks and look forward to an evening of rest. Ray made his way to his office, and along with the feelings of frustration, he felt deflated when he saw the pile of paperwork on his desk. As he sat down planning to spend an hour on the mountain, Sheila knocked on his door,

'Is there anything you want me to do?'

'Apart from you possibly being able to make this pile of papers disappear; you can get home with the others.'

'Ok, Ray, I will see you tomorrow.'

Ray had already decided that an hour would be long enough on the paperwork; he would like to get home to Jenny. She had mentioned in the morning that there was a dance she would like to go to if they were both home in time. He had not been able to promise anything but knew that he would like to go as well. As Sheila went out, he thought to himself that he knew nothing about her home life, and even though he kept a distance from his team he did know a little about each of them. He made a mental note that he would resolve this but knew it may have to wait till the case was finished. The time raced by and despite his best efforts the heap of papers didn't appear to diminish. He had just made the decision that enough was enough and the thought of dancing made him smile; so, got up to leave as Adam appeared at the door. Ray did his best but could not hide his sigh as Adam started to speak;

'Ray, sorry to interrupt you.'

This statement caused Ray to take a deep breath as Adam never spoke like that.

'That is fine, Sir; I was just getting ready to leave.'

Adam was soon back to his usual self and carried on speaking as though Ray had not spoken.

'I just wanted to see if you had any update for me on the case.'

Ray was quick enough to know what to say that would keep Adam happy.

'We have made some progress today; it is from forensics and has given us a connection between our 2nd victim and Steve Edwards.'

This was enough to make Adam smile and as always jump to conclusions.

'That is good news; so, it is all moving forward nicely.'

'Yes, Sir, I am hopeful we can move things on over the next few days. I was hoping to get away for the evening.'

'That is fine; just let the team know that I am happy with all the work they are doing.'

Ray thought he was finished but Adam then spoke again;

On a different note, Ray, I just wanted to let you know some details of a possible change.'

If asked Ray would have always answered that anything Adam said would never surprise him; this conversation did appear to be going that way. Before Ray could say anything, Adam continued:

'There is a strong possibility I am going to be moving on, a position has arisen at headquarters and I am being considered for the role.'

'I assume this is something you would like, Sir.'

Ray found it difficult to keep the sarcasm out of his voice, he felt the way Adam responded showed he had succeeded:

'Of course, it is a regional post and involves collating information from all the regional forces.'

Ray could fully understand the appeal to Adam as it sounded as though it would be a working day revolving around paperwork and figures.

'Well, good luck, Sir; when do you hope to hear?'

'It is still early days, but it has been mentioned they would like to get the role up and running as soon as possible. I will let you know more when I do.'

Then in quick succession, Adam took Ray by surprise again.

'I know we have had our differences over the years, but I have always respected you as an officer and your results speak for themselves. Whoever takes over from me has a good station and team to work with.'

Adam then told Ray he would see him in the morning and left his office. Once he was alone, Ray took a minute to digest this news. Adam was correct in that they had had differences over the years, though Ray was always happy in that he knew how to work around Adam and the many obstacles he would sometimes put in the way for Ray to get a result. He was then struck by the thought that currently, Adam pestered him in the station for recent figures, in the future he would be doing it from a distance but with the support of others at the Regional Head Office. Ray decided he would worry about working with a new Superintendent when it happened.

Ray's next thought turned to Jenny and the journey home; Adam had held him up from leaving but if he was lucky, he should get home in time. He had promised that if time allowed, they would go to dance this evening. This would be a new experience for Ray as the dance was outside the area so for the first time, he would be dancing in a room with people who did not know him. He knew that he was now a confident dancer but still got nervous about initially dancing in front of strangers. It did help when others had said to him that it was best to dance and think no-one was watching you.

The drive home was one of the better journeys he had made since he had started commuting; in that the traffic was light and there were no hold ups. He opened the front door as Jenny came down the stairs; he could do nothing to stop the grin spreading across his face. She was wearing a purple lace dress which was a favourite of his to see her in.

'That was worth the journey home for.'

'Thank you, I take it you approve?'

'You look lovely.'

'Well, you had better go and see if you can compete with me, then we can go out.'

'I couldn't even get close, but I will try my best.'

As he walked past to go upstairs, he placed a kiss on the end of her nose.

The evening was different in other ways to normal for Ray; this would be the first time they had been to a dance while he was working a case. Ray had learnt to relax more now than ever; the dancing classes were a part of this as well as the understanding from Jenny of his situation.

Once at the hall and being made welcome, Ray felt at ease as the music started, they returned to their seats after their first dance. Ray smiled awkwardly as the couple sat with them complimented him on his dancing. Unfortunately, as Ray always found as he relaxed the evening seemed to fly past, soon the organiser was thanking everyone for coming and announcing the last waltz. As they made their way to the car Jenny squeezed his hand and smiled;

'What is making you smile?

'Nothing really just thinking how lucky I am.'

'I think we are both lucky.'

Ray was determined that nothing was going to spoil his evening and made the effort to stay in a relaxed frame of mind. Despite his efforts, he was unable to switch off completely and while they had a coffee at home he said:

'What would your thoughts be on this case we have now?'

'Until you find this Jimmy Hammer, moving things forward will be difficult. It seems he has been involved from the beginning. It ties him in even more so in that he knew the 2nd victim as well. The train of thought could be he is the man responsible, or he could be at risk as he knows both of the others.'

'The thing I cannot understand is he is a seasoned criminal; so why are we finding it so hard to track him down?'

'Even you realise how easy it is for someone to make themselves invisible to others if they want to. You have the last known address from his prison records, but if since release he has kept out trouble, no one would follow up if he moves.'

Ray sighed:

'We just need that small percentage of luck to help move things along.'

Jenny was soon aware that if she allowed things to carry on; they would sit for hours discussing the case. She reached for his hand and smiled, pulling him slowly towards her.

'I think you should stop talking and give me a cuddle, he moved to her and kissed her as they stood up and he led her upstairs.

The buzz of the alarm shook Ray awake and he was surprised by how well he had slept. They had made love and he had drifted off into a deep sleep till the alarm rang.

They both had to get to work, so there was not a lot of time to carry on the conversation from the previous evening. Ray found he had plenty to think about on the journey to the station, he had still not got fully used to the idea of the time it took to get to work. Today was not helped by heavy rain and strong winds. This meant traffic moved slower than normal, so he did plenty of thinking. The first job was the morning briefing to see if anything had come in overnight; Ray always felt fortunate that though crime was around all the time, murder cases were infrequent, so this allowed the team to concentrate. His first job after the meeting was to go and meet with Steve Edward's sister Jean Daniels. He did not look forward to meetings like this but knew it had to be done.

The briefing followed the usual pattern with Ray pushing the team to uncover more information as they progressed through the day. This was something Ray had learnt from his time working with Steve when he first joined the team. Man, management was important in getting the best from everyone. All the team had their strong points but these were very different in them all; this meant treating them the same but also recognising they had differing needs. When this was first pointed out to Ray as he progressed in CID; he felt it was pandering to the team that he felt should all know their roles, he soon realised that the methods he was being shown worked and got the best out of everyone.

'I would like to think that when we meet up later; someone can give us some good news. So, get out on the streets and ask the questions you all know need asking.'

The team left the room quickly, all feeling that Ray was getting frustrated with the lack of information coming in. Sheila came forward knowing about the meeting with Jean.

'Sir, all the team are doing their best.'

'I know and I was not getting at them; just sometimes everyone needs a push to help them along.'

'As long as that is all it was, each of us needs to keep on top of our emotions as enquiries continue, especially when it involves one of our own. Do you want me to come with you this morning?'

Ray appreciated the input from Sheila and not for the first time he realised it was due in part to his relationship with Jenny; which caused him to look at things differently to in the past. If anyone had questioned his actions in the past, he would not have been pleased. He now knew that it was meant in a good way; as the team relied on him to keep them focused.

'I will make sure they know later; I was not having a moan at any of them. I would like you to stay here this morning, keeping an eye on things. Once they are all out and about; you could join them and fingers crossed you might find the piece of the puzzle that opens this up for us all.'

Sheila acknowledged this; and went to her desk. Ray had time before he was due to meet Jean at the railway station. The rain had stopped and the sun was now out; so, he decided he would walk through the park and meet the train, then they could come back for the car when Jean was ready to go to the house.

Chapter Ten

Ray had never met Jean properly; he had a memory of seeing her briefly at a work party with Steve. This meant he was going on some pictures from the house to recognise her by. He did not need to worry as he looked along the platform as the train allowed the passengers off. The woman he was looking at was a female version of Steve. He waited as she walked towards him.

'Mrs Daniels?'

'Yes, that is right, you must be D.I Keane. Please call me Jean.'

'It is nice to meet you, Jean, though I am sorry about the circumstances. You can call me Ray.'

'Thank you, Ray; Steve did talk about you. I must admit, I was shocked to hear the news. I always thought of the possibility of Steve getting injured or worse during his career. I never gave it a thought it would happen in retirement.'

'Unfortunately, sometimes the people we mix with can take time to act; and they can bear grudges for a long time.'

'I do not know if I can be of much help to you. When Steve moved to Norfolk our relationship mainly relied on phone calls.'

'I realise that it was more a case of you are his next of kin. There is the matter of the house to arrange along with personal things. I can take you to the house when you are ready,'

After Jean had explained that she was not comfortable staying at the house; Ray told her that they could arrange a room at the Old Inn in the village. By this time, they had reached the car park at the rear of the police station. The one thing that Ray hoped for was to get away from the station without being interrupted by Adam. He decided luck was on his side, when he recognised the car of the District Commissioner so knew Adam would be occupied; most probably telling him how close they were to closing the case.

Jean stopped outside the station and looked around at the area.

'I never visited here much when Steve was working; I didn't realise what the surroundings were like. It is difficult to put things together, nice weather and hearing the birds singing then people dying in horrible circumstances.'

Ray could see that she was looking out across the park, with Nelson Court in the background.

She added:

'It looks nice in the sunshine; even the flats.'

'They will certainly start to look better soon, there is big refurbishment going on as you can see. This should improve the outlook.'

Ray could see Jean thinking about what she had mentioned about crimes, and felt similar to how he always did when a conversation raised these points;

'It is the life we choose, and we can only do our best to keep things separate. This usually allows us to do what is needed to complete our work, it is not easy. The majority of the time we all manage; sometimes you just need the help of colleagues to get through.'

'I suppose in a different way it is like all walks of life. Except crime can have such an impact on all involved.'

'It certainly does; though as you say everyone can have things to deal with in life. Normally as well the cases we deal with have an impersonal feel. That is why this feels different, firstly because Steve was ex force; then secondly, I knew him as a friend as well.'

While talking to her Ray decided that he should spend time with Jean as she could find the next few days difficult.

'I shall take you over to the house, then show you some of the surrounding area.'

'That would be kind of you; I can spend three or four days here as I took time off work.'

'We shall do that then; I can be your transport for today; then some of the others can transport you about as needed. We can return here later, and you can meet the rest of the team.'

'Thank you.'

As he did not want to get tied up with Adam he rang from his mobile and left a message with the secretary of his plans for the day. He made a point of telling her that the team were all organised for the day with duties to perform. Ray was hoping that even if she did not feel she could help much; just by talking through about Steve since he retired might provide some information that would fit in with what they already knew.

Ray opened the car door for Jean, and they left the car park without interruptions, this always felt like an achievement for Ray. They made their way onto the one-way system and while he was driving, he asked Jean about her life.

Jean told him that her life had not been very exciting but was happy to let him know what it had involved.

She had moved to Leeds some years back; she never married but had a large circle of friends. She had worked as a librarian initially full time but now only part-time. When Steve had retired, she was tempted to move to Norfolk; but decided as she had a lot of friends in the area she would stay where she was. In the beginning, she had visited and Steve returned the visits but without any reason, these visits became less frequent.

'I am glad now that I stayed in Leeds, as I think I would be feeling very lonely now.'

'When you spoke to Steve did, he ever mention feeling threatened at all.'

'I would say no more than I expect you all do; especially when you have been in the job for any length of time. I do feel sad that Steve now had time to enjoy life but this has been taken away so abruptly.'

Ray could see that Jean was getting upset and as well as not wanting her to; he also knew she would be of no help while feeling like this. He drove on in silence for a while and allowed Jean to compose herself. After a time, Jean spoke again:

'Sorry about that; it is just getting used to the idea that I cannot pick up the phone and speak to him. He was the last link to any family we had.'

Ray was able to understand this in a different way as he thought back to when his wife Mary had passed away, it was the fact that out of the blue it would dawn on you that the person was gone.

'Are you ready to go to the house now?'

'I think so, I don't want to take up too much of your time.'

'It is okay for today; the team all know their roles and what is expected of them. I will have to be back at the station for the evening briefing. After we finish at the house, I will get things arranged for you at the Village Inn.'

'Thank you, I do appreciate all you are doing.'

'When you get to the house, I can leave you to your own thoughts. Though I will ask if as you look around if you notice anything unusual can you let me know. It will be difficult as our forensics team have already removed some pieces to be gone through.'

'I will do my best but cannot promise too much as on the odd occasions I visited I did not take much notice of possessions Steve had in the house.'

It was quieter at the house than in recent days, the only sign to the outside world of anything untoward was the crime scene tape at the front door. Ray parked the car on the driveway and walked Jean to the door. He moved the tape to one side and opened the door for her, stepping to one side to let her go in first. Jean stopped just inside the hallway.

'I have only been here a few times, but this feels wrong as though I am intruding on Steve's privacy.'

Ray went to speak then thought how harsh it would sound, but he thought that the one thing Steve no longer had was privacy.

'Just take your time; would you prefer me to wait in the car' Ray made this suggestion with a hopeful feeling. He was slightly disappointed when Jean replied:

'I would rather not be alone in the house.'

His disappointment was out of the knowledge that he could not do anything to help in the house.

Ray was having to fight with himself to keep his emotions in check. He knew that Jean would take time to look at things, but he could not help feeling frustrated. He wanted to get on; even though he was aware there was little he could do that the team were not already working on. His frustration was getting unbearable when he was brought back to the room by Jean speaking:

'I cannot be sure but there is one thing missing I think from his desk.'

Ray was surprised as it had not looked initially and still did not look as though the interior of the house had been disturbed.

'Sorry Jean, what is that then?'

'His pocket watch from his retirement.'

Ray was transported back by his thoughts and remembered that Steve had a thing about collecting watches. This meant it had been obvious to them all; for his retirement present to be an engraved pocket watch, to add to his collection. He did recall at the time being amazed at the cost of the watch; at the same time, he remembered how impressed Steve had been with his present.

'I remember now he liked his watches.'

'Yes, he rang me after the party and made a point of saying how pleased he was with it. I never understood his passion for collecting, but he always enjoyed talking about them.'

'This could be a help; I will get some officers over and they can go through again; to see if it looks as if anything is missing.'

'Tell them to look for imprints in the dust.'

Ray could see that Jean wondered from his expression what she meant.

'Steve was like our mum, when he did housework, he had a tendency to dust around items rather than moving them.'

Ray smiled and also thought how quick Jenny would comment if he tried that.

'I will tell them that; I wonder if that watch was stolen as a way of a point being made.'

'I do not think like a police officer. I suppose it could have been.

Again, Ray could not help but smile:

'Sorry Jean; I was just thinking out loud. If you are ready, let me get you to the Village Inn and get you settled. You can always can come back to the house again. Being his only relative, and given we are nearly finished here, if there is anything you would like to take home with you it would be okay.'

Jean had not given it much thought that she would now be responsible for arranging the clearance of all the belongings and the house.

Ray could hear Jean saying thank you; but already his mind was wandering over these new details. Thinking it through about the watch got his brain in gear to working out was there some point to the act. Possibly suggesting was it a Time for Revenge.

Chapter Eleven

Ray found it increasingly difficult to concentrate over the following minutes; as he was busy getting Jean to the Village Inn. While this was going on, he was doing his best to be polite; but was eager to get back to the station feeling the need to pass on the information regarding the watch. This could be the first link to the puzzle as to what had occurred and could also show the connection to the other crime at the church. That link was obscure but the body at the church had been found on the stairs leading to the clock tower so again was the link to do with time.

Once he was happy that Jean was settled, he told her they would speak in the morning. Then he made his way back to King's Lynn, on his way he rang; telling the desk sergeant he was to make a radio call out to all the team to be at the office when he arrived.

There was a buzz of excitement like a charge of electricity going around the room; when Ray walked in. The team all felt something must have happened for them to get the call back as they had. Initially, Ray was disappointed in the response from the room, as he told them about the missing pocket watch.

'I realise it is not a lot to go on. Though it does give us a lead to work with, something that we have not had before. If the person who killed Steve took this watch, they may try to sell it on.'

This comment brought a suitable reaction from the rest and pleased Ray that they were starting to see what he did. Some of the team had been with him for a time now, but with different situations, it meant this was the first time for a few to be working closely with Ray. He had persuaded Adam to give them some officers attached from uniform; this would free up the C.I.D officers to be on the streets.

'I know time is getting on; so, first thing tomorrow I want two of you over at the house.'

This brought another groan from the team as they did not see how there was anything else to gain from that line of enquiry. Ray carried on talking and it did raise a ripple of laughter when he explained to them about looking for things that were missing; that the giveaway could be a dust mark.

'Tim, I want you to start visiting the pawn shops to see if anyone has tried to trade in the pocket watch. It will be distinctive due to the engraving.'

As usual, Ray was impressed by Tim as he responded quickly;

'I think I saw some pictures at the house from the retirement party, one of which might show us the watch.'

'Quick thinking, Tim; if possible, visit the house this evening, so you have the photo with you first thing.'

'Okay, unless anyone has any other news to pass on, let us call it a day for now; see you all in the morning.'

As Ray was getting ready to leave his office, having phoned and brought Adam up to date with things; his phone rang again. For a brief moment he thought of leaving it; the fact this was not in his nature meant he picked up the receiver. Silently cursing under his breath, he answered;

'D.I. Keane.'

Lisa replied:

'I hope you will sound happier than that in a moment.'

'Sorry, Lisa, how can you help me?'

Lisa laughed at the fact that Ray had already assumed she was going to help.

'I think you are correct in that I think I am going to be of help; the small piece of material you thought so little of.'

Ray felt himself take an intake of breath, was he about to get another piece of the puzzle.

'We found a small sample of DNA on it. It is a possible match for Jimmy Hammer.'

'You say a possible match.'

'Only because the DNA on file for him, was collected when he was first in trouble. And though it does not change, I would prefer another sample to match with. Unfortunately, it does not work like the films, in that we can just say it must be his.'

'So, we still need to find him then for differing reasons.'

'Looks like it sorry.'

'No, it is not your problem, thanks for the science helping us.'

Ray felt as though it was a case of one step forward then two back. He also knew that in the modern world the Crown Prosecution Service always wanted to be as sure as possible before taking a case to court. He had to be as positive as possible in that they at least had a name and a connection to the crimes. Even if the person was being very difficult to track down; he knew that they would eventually find him.

For the first time since they had moved the journey home was extremely frustrating. The traffic was moving slowly Ray found himself thinking about how the case was going. He always found that thinking things through on his own could go two ways; it could be the lightbulb moment in him solving issues or as was now he just felt it was no further forward than when the initial call had been taken. Fortunately, as he pulled into the drive; Jenny was just getting out of her car. This brought a smile to his face and he felt himself relax. Jenny had just recently returned to work after some holiday while they had moved; she was pleased with how she had been made welcome at the new station even though she realised it was early days and her superiors would be watching to see how she performed.

'Hello, Sweetheart; you look as though you are ready for a drink.'

'That would be lovely, after the day I have had plus the journey home I am ready for it.'

They went inside and Ray was still surprised by how coming home made him feel. It was a decision he had not made lightly to move out of the town and then have to commute every day, but he was sure it had been the right choice. They stood in the kitchen doorway and kissed then Jenny spoke:

'Stew for dinner; will be ready in about half an hour.'

'Great just time to have a shower and change.'

There were always a few evenings a week, where they would be indoors; with no plans to go out. Tonight, was one such evening so after dinner; they both sat and tried to unwind. As much as Ray did not like to discuss work while at home it would normally find itself being talked of.

'So how was your day then?'

'I am still just finding my feet really. There are no major incidents at the moment, I have been paired with a D.C. who has been taking me around the area.'

The evening passed pleasantly and as usual with nothing to deal with; Ray sat and read then fell asleep in the chair. He was always amazed how that if they went out, he was fine, but sitting still did not do him any good. He woke up as Jenny nudged him and suggested going to bed. One good thing to have come from being more relaxed with life as he did sleep better. Before he knew it, the alarm was buzzing to signal another day.

Ray's thoughts on the journey to work; were if the team had struggled to be positive about the missing watch. They would be less than thrilled with the information from Lisa. He had, to tell them this news at the morning briefing.

He walked in and was not surprised to see everyone was already at their desks, some even working at their computers. The one thing he could have done without was the appearance of Adam at the door.

'Carry on, Inspector.' Was all Adam said; this meant that Ray had to go straight on with things without speaking to anyone first.

'Right listen up, you know the roles for today. Those going to the house make sure you are meticulous, look over everything. So, you are all aware; I had a call from Lisa late yesterday. There is a DNA match from the small piece of material found at the church.'

Initially, Ray could sense the anticipation; he knew it wouldn't last, and he really did not want any input especially from Adam. He carried on without giving anyone time to interrupt,

'The problem we will have is getting enough details to convince the CPS. The sample is small and even though the DNA match is there, Lisa would like a new sample from the person to compare.

From the back of the room Adam coughed:

'So, do you have a name for everyone?'

Ray did his best to avoid a sarcastic answer:

'Yes, it was brought up on the system, Jimmy Hammer.'

If the team was not already holding their breath, they were now.

'Before you all get excited, can I just point out; we still have to find Jimmy. This now has to be our priority.

Ray had to admit the next question from the room took him by surprise:

'Where do we look as he seems to have disappeared.'

Before he answered he took a moment; he knew the P.C asking had been seconded by Adam to help out, so did not want his answer to knock anyone's confidence or even upset Adam too much.

'We all look everywhere; we already have looked then look further afield if necessary.'

The picture of Jimmy from his last prison term, as well as being circulated locally had also been sent out to neighbouring forces.

'Someone knows where he is; going on past experiences, he like a lot of serial criminals will have people willing to hide him.'

To Ray as he spoke it sounded like something out of a book but it was proven time and again this did happen.

'Now, come on; you all know what you need to be doing so, get on and good luck.'

The morning was full of surprises for Ray when he looked up and saw that Adam had left the room. This was very unlike him as he usually liked to talk to Ray in the morning; as he would hope to hear good news regarding progress. Ray could not help but feel this change was down to the possible move but was still surprised as he knew that Adam would like to finish his time at King's Lynn with another success to speak to the press about. The team made their way to the respective duties, Sheila came up to speak:

'So, how far forward do you think we are?'

'I am convinced that Jimmy is our man; I would think our best hope in locating him is if he tries to sell the watch.'

'What if he just sells it in a local pub, which could be easier.'

'I agree, but even he will realise the value of it; I guarantee he will want to get as much as possible for it.'

While they were talking, Ray could not help but also think that Jimmy had moved out of the area, This would make finding him harder, the background checks they had carried out all revealed that he had no family anywhere. Which then meant even for a hardened criminal he had no ties to any place.

'What about if he is holed up with some friends?'

Ray had noticed recently that Sheila had started to think along the same lines as he did. This, did make his job feel easier as he did not have to spend time explaining everything in detail.

'What we know so far is the word friends would be pushing it, he may have acquaintances. I think from the checks the only possible friend is currently a guest of the mortuary. There is certainly no family Mum and Dad are both dead so he could be anywhere.'

'I will start calling other forces, possibly even further afield than already covered; also get his picture circulated we need to find him.'

'You do not need to tell me that.'

Neither of them knew that Jimmy would be closer than they thought by the end of the day. He would be having to hide well once he saw the papers.

Chapter Twelve

At that moment Jimmy was sat at a seat in the rear of a roadside café. He had no real idea of the hunt that was going on for him, he knew enough that the police would be looking for him but so far press coverage had only been local. Since leaving the body of Jeff in the church tower, Jimmy had been out of the area. He had had access to a car which as far as he knew the police did not know about. He would agree with the thoughts of D.I. Keane in that the word friends meant very little; the people Jimmy had mixed with recently would only appear friendly if there was something in it for them. Occasionally after the past few days, he thought about Jeff and was slightly upset with what had happened; Jeff had always been around when they were younger and Jimmy had felt sorry for him mainly because of how his mum was with him. Then cruelly Jimmy would think well now the apron strings were well and truly cut.

Jimmy would tell anyone who would listen that even though he was fully aware that he was a criminal; until recently he had only committed crimes to get by. This was true to the point that he never hurt anyone personally, a lot of the time since he had first encountered Steve Edwards his crimes had been stealing. A lot of the time it was taking the opportunity of an open door to burgle a house then sell on anything he got hold of. After his first spell in prison, then seeing that he could make money by passing information to Steve. Jimmy had always put some money away in case he needed it; the last few days he had certainly needed it. Once he had dealt with the problems, he could see Jeff causing; Jimmy had made his way north. He ended up in Scarborough and it was only as he parked the car in a side street; did he stop and think that this place was the one time he had been happy. It was not a regular occurrence but the family had gone on holiday to Scarborough. He remembered they had stayed in a caravan and he recalled him and his sister running around on the beach; and all the lights and noise of the arcades along the seafront. Even though this had been a good time Jimmy always felt sad whenever he thought of Julie; she had died in an accident when riding her bike in the street. Mum and Dad had never been what you would call great parents but it was all downhill after the accident. His mum had slowly drunk herself to death and he never really grasped what was happening but his dad just appeared to give up.

Jimmy mentally shook himself back to reality; he knew exactly how much trouble he was in, all he could think about was how to avoid the police. He knew this would be difficult and despite what people might think disappearing out of the country was not as simple as that.

As he would eventually find out, the reason behind him deciding to kill Steve was not true. Jimmy had never used violence in any crime. When he heard through the grapevine of prison gatherings that Steve Edwards had retired and was going to write a book, the rumours were that the main focus of this book was to be of the time Steve had spent in the police force and as well as documenting the changes he had seen over the years. The information that took Jimmy by surprise was that Steve would reveal how he had got a lot of the information that had helped solve a majority of his cases. Jimmy had never really thought of himself as a grass, but was well aware there were several people in various prisons that had been given long sentences due to the information he had passed to Steve. He knew full well the contacts these people had who would happily inflict a lot of pain on Jimmy if the money was right.

Unfortunately listening to rumours that circulated very quickly in a prison environment did no-one any good; invariably there was no truth in them, and a lot of time it was just gossip to pass the time or to keep others anxiously looking over their shoulders.

Jimmy had been released a few weeks now but he still harboured thoughts as to what to do about the possibility of his name appearing in a book. He had skirted around the problem; when talking to his parole officer, to see if that brought forth any answers. He was sensible enough to realise the benefits of having a parole officer on his side. However, these conversations never revealed a suitable answer. The one thing that would have saved Steve's life was if Jimmy had not listened to the rumours or better still tried talking to Steve. The truth of the matter was yes Steve was writing a book, but he was fully aware of what would happen to anyone from the criminal fraternity if they were known to pass information to the police. Depending on the seriousness of the matter, the grass could be given false information to pass along, which would then make them unreliable to anyone, or matters would be dealt with controlled by someone with a lot more influence than a petty criminal. The other problem with the situation for the police officer concerned was it could leave them open to blackmail or worse; this was the reason why no names would ever appear in print.

In the short time since his release apart from the obvious crimes committed, Jimmy had soon returned to his old habits, and took advantage of the nice weather. There was not a criminal anywhere who would say they understood the mentality of people to leave doors and windows open just because the sun was out. In as much as you could think people should not touch stuff that doesn't belong to them; that unfortunately is not human nature for some.

So far Jimmy had managed to steal a very nice radio and several wallets, these had just been left on surfaces just inside open doors. The chance for revenge on Steve Edwards came about in two ways. Firstly, Jimmy met Jeff in a local pub; even though Jeff knew how Jimmy's life had panned out, he still felt that they were friends. It would have been from the point of view of a psychologist that Jeff enjoyed being in the company of Jimmy; mainly because his home life was not great. In the modern world, the idea always seemed to be to look for someone to blame and, in most cases, it would be the statement Blame the Parents that was becoming quite normal.

Jeff if asked would tell it differently; he really did not care about what his parents thought and had spent the majority of the time the last few years thinking of ways to get out of the family home. His father had never shown much affection towards his son; as though in some way to make up for this his mum totally spoilt him. He had lost count of the number of times he had sat as a youngster; being embarrassed by listening to his mum tell anyone who would listen how clever her young man was and what great things were in store for him. He had sat in his bedroom for many evenings going through things in his mind as to how he could leave home. When it happened, it was nothing dramatic at all, his dad was at the pub and his mum was at one of her many meetings. Jeff threw some clothes in a holdall, took what money he had plus some out of a tin; that his mum was convinced no-one knew about; and then walked out of the house and shut the door on that part of his life.

Despite staying close to the area and his mum pestering people to ask if they had seen her son, Jeff stayed out of his parents' sight, not that his dad was making a huge effort to look for him. It was when his dad went to identify the body that he saw his son for the first time in two years. His dad showed the first signs of any emotion at this moment; they had already had the body identified; this was just a mere formality. At the time Ray thought of it as a chance for the man to show his feelings for Jeff.

When Jimmy met Jeff in the back room of the pub; he was also surprised as he had not seen him since before, he went to prison. They said hello and agreed on having a drink, as they chatted Jimmy felt relaxed for the first time in a long while.

'Do you remember that copper who first arrested you?'

'Yeah, I always felt he was okay for a copper.'

'Well, he is retired now and lives in the village.'

'Really I never knew exactly where he lived, perhaps I could pay him a visit.'

'You are not thinking of doing anything silly are you; not having recently got out of prison.'

'You are well informed ain't you.'

'Well, I keep my ears open.'

'Still living at home with Mummy.' sniped Jimmy.

At this comment, Jeff got up and walked out of the pub. As it was busy no-one took any notice; even though no-one realised this would be the last time they would see Jeff alive.

Again, with no-one bothering about anything but their drinks or whose throw of the darts it was next; Jimmy followed Jeff outside. For a brief moment he thought he had lost him as there was no sign of him; then he ran to catch up as he saw him cross the road and go into the churchyard via a small side gate. At the far end of the church was an old building that was covered in moss and did not look as though it had been used in years. Jimmy stood and watched as Jeff moved some wood to one side and went in. He walked quickly across and followed Jeff in; he was surprised to see it was laid out with an old camp bed and a few other bits.

'How long have you been living like this?'

'A while now; as far as I know, no-one has seen me coming or going. I try to avoid contact with others.'

Jeff was right in that no-one had seen his movements or else someone would have told his mum. He went on to explain about walking out of the house and how he had been living for the last few months; even Jimmy was taken aback that no-one had seen him or found out about the shed.

'So, what have you planned next then?'

'I'm not sure; I have literally taken each day as it comes. When I first walked out, I wanted to get as far away as I could. Then as time went on, I realised no-one took any notice of me.'

Jimmy who had lived rough many times in the past knew it was not easy, but he also knew how Jeff had survived like he had.

'How about I get us some drinks and I will stay here with you.'

'I don't want anything else to drink, but you are welcome to stay if you want.'

Jimmy saw this as a way of solving a problem at that moment of somewhere to stay, without realising that over the next few days how necessary it would become. The two of them sat talking for most of the night; Jimmy did end up feeling sorry for Jeff. While they were talking Jimmy also got to think more about Steve and how his career had progressed; with the help for a small amount of payment of the information Jimmy had passed on. As the night wore on, they both fell asleep with different thoughts in their minds.

Jeff was thinking how good it was to have a friend again. While Jimmy had the idea on how he could get some form of revenge on Steve; even with the niggling thought in the far recess of his brain that he had no cause for revenge.

The next morning Jimmy left before Jeff was awake and went for a walk around the village. he had no idea where Steve Edwards lived but by pure chance, he found out; as he walked along the edge of the playing field by the cricket ground. He saw Steve walk out of his driveway, Jimmy quickly ducked behind the hedge. Now that Jimmy knew where Steve lived, he could feel a red mist of anger descend over him. This did not improve as he looked at the nice house and thought how cheaply he had passed information over. He watched carefully from his hiding place as Steve went to the side of the house. He saw him walk through a gate that obviously led to the back garden. An idea started to form as he watched, he would come back later and wait to see if Steve went out and then he would have a look around. He made his way back to the church to see what Jeff was doing; when he got there, he saw several people milling about so decided against going any further.

This interruption led him to move quicker on a new plan for revenge than he had first thought of. He made his way back to the spot at the cricket ground and settled down to wait. Unfortunately for Steve the longer Jimmy waited the more he kept thinking about how to gain a payback. Jimmy was just thinking about moving and almost deciding it was a waste of time; when Steve came out of the house and walked to his car. It was quiet in the area and Jimmy could hear the phone conversation Steve was having, he was arranging to meet someone in 30 minutes. Suddenly Jimmy saw his chance; he waited for Steve to leave in the car, then for safety he waited another five minutes. Then with a confident air about him, Jimmy walked up to the side gate. Something he had learned very early on in his life; was that if you looked as though you belonged no-one took much notice of you. The other thing in his favour was as he thought of it a village mentality; which was people who had lived in the area all their lives still did not lock everywhere up. The side gate opened easily and without a single creak of a hinge. The garden could only be described as immaculate; Jimmy scanned the area quickly and made a mental note of things on the patio, and then saw the French doors that led into the house. He had nothing else in mind for now and again with confidence walked back out onto the main road, almost bumping into Jeff who was walking past.

'What are you doing, Jimmy?'

'Who are you, my mother?'

'No, but I wondered where you had got to.'

'Well now you know; don't start sticking your nose into my business.'

Again, as in the pub; Jeff took this comment to heart and just turned away and walked off. Jimmy was tempted to follow him, but decided against it the fewer people he saw the better. This latest run in with Jeff made Jimmy decide if he was going to do anything about Steve it needed doing quick. He didn't think Jeff would do anything to draw attention to himself, but didn't want to take the chance of him talking to anyone about having met Jimmy.

He made his mind up he would surprise Steve later today then at least that would be dealt with; even though he still had no idea what he was going to do or how badly things were going to end up. Jimmy made his way back to his hiding spot behind the hedgerow; opposite the house and settled down to wait for Steve to return. He didn't have long to wait, Steve pulled into his driveway and got out of the car; he walked to the side gate. Jimmy could hear him laughing at something that had been said on his phone. As he watched Steve walk in through the gate there was the feeling of a switch being moved in Jimmy's mind as he followed the route across the road towards the gate. He slowly opened the gate and was surprised to see Steve leaning over a flower bed. With no real thought of what he was doing; Jimmy picked up a spade, he would comment later that the idea was just to hit Steve across the back. He stepped across the grass towards Steve as Steve turned around; Steve looked up with a smile of recognition, in a brief second Jimmy interpreted this as a smirk:

'Hello, Jimmy, long time no see.'

There was no reply from Jimmy; he lifted the spade and swung it viciously towards Steve. As Steve went to move out of the way, it connected with a dull thud to the side of his head; this action seemed to kick off a rage in Jimmy. Even as Steve was falling sideways into the flowers Jimmy rained blows onto his head. Funnily as Jimmy looked around at the perfect garden, he thought how upset Steve would be about the mess in the flowerbed. The rage passed almost as quickly as it had surfaced; Jimmy looked down at the mess that was Steve's head and quickly turned away. He moved towards the gate; then slowed as he saw the doors were open. His criminal mind kicked in fully and thought I am already in deep trouble; I might as well see if I can get anything out of this. He walked into the room and scanned everywhere with his eyes moving furiously around. He was instantly drawn like a Magpie to the shine of the glass on the pocket watch; even his untrained eye knew it was worth a bit.

He picked up the watch; then decided it was time to get out. It was only as he went to walk out did, he notices the blood that had obviously spattered on to his clothes. Looking around quickly he saw the coats on the hooks by the door. Without thinking too much he grabbed an overcoat and put it on. It was too big but the benefit was that it covered his clothes completely. He continuously scanned around as he walked back out the way he had entered not more than 15 minutes ago; fortunately for Jimmy, the house was not overlooked by any of the neighbours. As he had made his way out the realisation of what had happened kicked in and he started to shake. Luck appeared to be with him as, despite the shaking, instinct took over and, on his way, out Jimmy picked up the spade which had become a murder weapon from the lawn where he had dropped it. Holding it closely by his side he made his way along the road. He knew he had to get out of sight as soon as possible and even though it must have looked weird that on a nice summer's day a person was walking around in an overcoat, there was no-one around who took any notice. As if on automatic pilot; Jimmy made his way to the shed in the churchyard where Jeff was living. Pushing some of the moss to one side he went in and was sure no-one had seen him. It was just a brief moment of time for his eyes to adjust to the gloom and realise Jeff was not about, he jumped as the door scrapped open again and in walked Jeff.

'What have you been up to? That coat is not yours, is it?'

'Stop with all the questions will you.'

Jeff moved away slightly as he saw how angry Jimmy was; also, there was a glaze about his eyes that Jeff found he couldn't look at. Jimmy slowly felt his heart stop racing.

'Look, sorry, I just don't like answering questions all the time.'

Then Jeff saw the spade Jimmy was holding; fortunately for Jimmy due to the lack of light in the shed, Jeff couldn't see the blood on the edge of the spade.

'Why have you got a spade?'

Sarcastically Jimmy replied;

'I thought I would do some gardening.'

'Very funny.'

'You know me always good for a laugh; I just happened to see it resting against a gate so I picked it up. You know the saying, old habits die hard.'

As he finished speaking; Jimmy put the spade against the wall; Jeff didn't fail to notice that he made sure it was put behind some other old stuff as though he was hiding it. The next shock for Jeff was when Jimmy took off the coat; the blood that had spattered his shirt was now drying but still obvious as to what it was.

'Sorry, more questions, is that blood on you?'

'Oh, that is nothing, I caught my arms on some brambles that is all. Have you got another shirt I can use?'

For an unexplained reason, Jeff decided he didn't want to know anymore; he threw a t-shirt towards Jimmy and then sat on his makeshift bed saying nothing but thinking a lot. After changing his shirt and trying to make conversation which failed; Jimmy sat and reflected on the events that had just happened. His first instinct was that he had to get out of the area; for some reason, he didn't want anything else to alarm Jeff. His thoughts were, he could lay low for a day or so and then make his move. As seemed to be happening a lot lately any plans Jimmy had seemed to change very quickly, and this was the same now things would get even worse over the next 48 hours. After a very strained evening and night in which Jeff had gone off somewhere; as soon as he came back, he started asking questions as if while he had been gone, he had built up the courage to ask more.

'Look Jeff, stop hassling me. You must have heard it before; but the less you know the better.'

Jeff went to speak but again when he looked at Jimmy, something stopped him. As time passed the information Jeff was going to hear was going to shock him even more. After two days of not leaving the shed Jimmy started to relax; he thought at the least he would have by now heard sirens in the village if nothing else. Then that morning, if possible, things did get worse.

Jeff burst into the shed with a look of astonishment on his face.

'What the hell is the matter with you?'

'The police have been called according to the gossip I just heard in the village; the body of Steve Edwards has been found; nothing to do with you, is it?'

'Don't be stupid; why would it be me?'

'Well, you are the one who had blood on them the other day.'

Many times, in the past the expression of a red mist descending had been used in association with Jimmy; this was exactly what happened again. He leapt across to Jeff and they both fell to the ground. For a brief moment, the wind was knocked from them both; just as quickly Jeff surprised him by starting to fight back. The struggle didn't last long as Jimmy was heavier and stronger than Jeff; after exchanging a few punches they separated and Jimmy thought that he had got the better of the situation. Suddenly Jeff sprung across and grabbed him again; more by luck he had hold of Jimmy by the throat. Having been in fights before a survival instinct kicked in for Jimmy. He lashed out and punched Jeff on the side of the head; then reached out his hand to see if he could find a weapon. His hand closed around a screwdriver; with not thought of his actions he stabbed at Jeff. There was a horrible gurgling sound and Jeff's body fell limply to one side. Jimmy made no attempt to move at first; then he threw down the screwdriver and moved closer to Jeff's lifeless body. He knew he had killed again but still felt for a pulse. Then he looked down at Jeff and spoke quietly:

'Now look what you made me do.'

As though he was proving to himself that he had a conscience, for what seemed a long time Jimmy sat and looked at the body of the one person he would always think of as a friend.

Slowly he was brought back to the present; was relieved to feel that he was thinking straight. He knew he had to move the body as he felt if it was found here; due to forensics, they would find something to link him to the place. An idea formed in his mind and even when the full implications of what he planned fell into place he felt sick but knew it had to be done. With no idea of time, he was taken back when he looked cautiously outside and it was getting dark. He grabbed the body under the arms then pulled it toward the entrance. Saying someone in his position would think straight would not sound normal; suddenly though Jimmy felt he had to do something to make this death seem weird, and possibly not connect with Steve. Jimmy found an old chisel in the corner and looking only to check he was in the right place he hacked at Jeff's wrist until the hand became detached. It would all become clear later that even he was surprised by how he was thinking. Going outside and seeing no-one around he went to the old door of the tower; knowing the stairs here led to the bells of the church. It was easy to force the old lock and slowly Jimmy placed things ready for anyone to find but thinking it would have no way of coming back to him.

Under the cover of darkness, Jimmy left the area without a thought for Steve or Jeff. Unfortunately for him due to the unstable situation, he also gave no thought to the coat or spade still in the shed.

Chapter Thirteen

Ever since his first day at cadet training college; Ray had understood that police work was different in so many ways. As he progressed through the ranks; nothing had happened to make him change his mind on this. All crimes involved the same things he felt; when coming down to them being solved. The mantra Ray had learnt early on; he still passed on when talking to anyone in particular new members of his team. This was that police work and importantly successfully solving a crime came down to two things; firstly, a lot of hard graft from everyone involved, secondly a dose of good luck. He always liked to use an example of a police officer coming across a burglar walking out of a house with stolen property on him it was pure good luck. As another example he gave the team was his first big case which involved the footballer Joe Kipper; his killer was brought to justice when two traffic cops had stopped his car due to it having faulty rear lights.

This training meant that as Ray stood at the front of the room for the morning briefing and looked at everyone. He knew that as well as all the work being put in; they needed the help that a bit of luck would bring. The main point for Ray to make was to get it across to the team; they need to keep working at full speed to answer the many questions, this, in turn, would solve the crimes. The luck they needed would eventually show itself and fit in to the puzzle. The problem now was time. The longer it took initially to find information, or in their case a person; the harder it would become. The saving grace for him was the fact that Steve was one of their own; and even though Ray would never put any murder in a privileged category, it did have a bearing on the team. He was also acutely aware he would soon start to get pressure from Adam on how things were progressing, and Adam would not be able to help himself; he would mention budgets. As he looked around the room, he was pleased to see that everyone was looking alert; he knew the problems that cases could cause as time wore on. People would start to get tired and there were lots of examples of things being missed due to an officer not being fully aware of things. As was usual Ray only needed to stand at the front of the room and clear his throat; to get the attention of everyone. Just before he spoke, he was again surprised to see Adam stood just inside the door at the back.

'Good morning, all; I feel that today is important in the time scale of things. We are now approaching a week since the discovery of the second body.'

Ray continued for a few minutes; explaining that even though the connection was very tenuous he certainly felt the cases were linked.

'I cannot stress enough we need to find Jimmy Hammer. Tim, did you have any joy with the pawn shops and the watch?'

'Not yet, Sir; I have a person to visit today, his name is Joe Bloggs.'

After the laughter had spread around the room, everyone fell silent again as Adam coughed from his position at the doorway.

'Carry on Tim.'

'Thanks, I thought the same when given the name; but apparently, he is not officially listed. But will help people out with things that are not always what they seem.'

Tim had got Joe's name from a pawn shop in town. The owner had explained that taking items that were engraved with a name; made them difficult to sell on if needed. When Tim had decided to let the shop owner know he really needed to find the watch, without giving too much information they suggested he try Joe.

'So where will you find Mr Bloggs?'

'He operates from a shed in his house over at Sutton Bridge.'

'Right, I will leave you to deal with that. The rest of you I want out on the streets. You all have pictures of Jimmy and the watch, get the photos seen by as many people as possible.'

As had happened previously when Ray indicated the meeting was over, he looked up and saw that Adam had already left. He decided he would go and see him; before doing anything else. He had a feeling he could not explain, but he just thought something was not right. As he went to leave Sheila moved beside him.

'Where would you like me to start this morning?'

'I am going to leave you to co-ordinate things in the town. I want to see Adam, then I am going to go and go over things in the village.'

'You are going to see Adam voluntarily?'

118

'I know it is unusual but there is something on his mind and I would like to know what it is.'

'Most probably to do with his move.'

This took Ray slightly by surprise, he knew how gossip spread in the station, but hadn't thought that anyone else was aware of Adam leaving. Sheila had moved away to her desk and was organising things to keep in touch with the team as they were out and about.

Ray made his way to the second floor and the office suite; Adam had made his own over the last few years. His secretary looked up and also couldn't hide her surprise at seeing Ray;

'Good morning D.I. Keane, you do not have an appointment, do you?'

'No, I just wanted to have a quick word, before I carry on for the morning.'

'I will just check he is free.'

Ray always felt that Natasha as Adam's secretary was a line of defence, to not allow certain people in to see Adam. He waited patiently without showing his frustration.

'You can go in now.'

Ray smiled and said thanks while doing his best to keep any sarcasm out of his voice.

'Good morning, Sir. I just wondered if you had something on your mind; as you are showing up at the briefings but it is unusual you have nothing to say.'

'I thought that was how you liked it.'

Ray smiled,

'I do; but when it feels as though you are changing the habits of a lifetime Sir; it is a bit disconcerting.'

'It is good to know; I can still keep you on your toes.'

Adam then went on to explain that his move to headquarters was moving forward quickly.

'I have been keeping an eye on all ongoing cases; as I feel personally it would be good to get as many results as possible before I leave.'

'Myself and the team would like nothing better than to get the case solved as quickly as possible Sir. Though currently it is not proving very easy.'

Ray gave Adam all the details regarding the information, they had gathered so far. And even though Adam had surprised him in the past; he managed to do so again with his next statement.

'I will call some of the neighbouring Superintendents and see if we can move forward with their help.'

'Thank you, Sir.'

'Also, before you go, even though there has been some gossip around the station; I will be making an official announcement about my future at the end of the week.'

Ray felt that he just wanted to get on with things; but could also tell that Adam wanted to talk more.

'Any news on a replacement yet, Sir?'

'Not yet; I do not think they will hurry as it can all be monitored from head office. Though I have heard there are three or four names in the picture.'

This did not exactly inspire Ray the fact that Adam was leaving but could still be in a position to oversee what was happening in the station. He knew they were already monitored by headquarters, but at least he knew where Adam was at present.

'I just wanted to know that everything was okay Sir. I will get on now and speak to you later.'

Ray went straight from the office to his car and made the short journey to Terrington St Clement. Village life had soon reverted to normal after the initial time of police everywhere, and other investigating teams being around. The local press had covered the story and it had slowly made its way into the national press, so far none of them had seen it necessary to send any reporters, in the modern world of social media so much more information was available without people needing to leave their offices. Ray parked his car at the playing field, and gave the house opposite a cursory glance. He started to walk towards the church and found that walking around gave him time to think. Over the years anyone who worked with him, had got to know that often during a case; Ray would take himself off somewhere and spend time alone working things through in his mind.

His main thought patterns at the moment, revolved around the urgency to locate Jimmy Hammer. He knew how easy it was for people if they needed to, to disappear from sight, but still found it hard to comprehend that in this day and age of surveillance, that someone who was known to the authorities as Jimmy was could essentially just vanish. Recently Jimmy had been tracked by the police, then the prison service and finally parole officers. He could understand the pressure from all the organisations linked to human rights groups put on the authorities, but surely even they could see that someone who was a serial criminal should have been kept a better check on. As he walked around what was a lovely village when the time was there to appreciate it, he was surprised by how busy it was. He had been to the spot several times over the years, but it had always been as part of an investigation so he had never had time to take a lot of notice of the area. Walking around he did think to himself that a lot of people especially the ladies; must all look quite immaculate as he saw several hair salons in 1 street. As he approached the end of his circuit of the village, he saw P.C. John Ford walking towards him.

'Good morning, Sir, I didn't expect to see you today.'

'I just came over to get a feel of the village for myself; I find it helps sometimes, especially once things have settled down a bit.'

'I was just carrying out a morning patrol. I have always tried to keep a routine of walking the village, and I know currently people have commented they like to see my presence.'

Ray was happy that he had had some time alone so said;

'I might join you for a while.'

Ray also saw an opportunity to get John's take on things. As they continued on their way Ray could see by people's reaction how they appreciated John being there.

'That is a blast from the past isn't it'

This comment came from Ray as they walked past Marshland Stores, to him it was a traditional hardware store. The window display carried various items from gardening to home interiors, outside on the pathway were wheelbarrows and BBQ equipment.

'The store has been in the family for years; it is the sort of place where you can just about get anything you need from a couple of screws to most things for a party.'

As they walked past John said hello and introduced Ray.

'This is Linda who owns the shop.'

'Good morning, I may have to visit soon as we are decorating our house.'

'You would be welcome. Are you any closer to finding out what happened to Steve?'

'We are gathering lots of information which will help us. Did you know him?'

'Only in passing as a customer; he was always interested in our gardening equipment.'

They stood chatting for a few minutes more, then Linda said:

'I will let you get on; hopefully, you will soon catch whoever was responsible for this horrible crime.'

As they walked away Ray found himself thinking of how society perceived things. In the time they had been talking; no mention had been made about the discovery of Jeff's body. Yet both crimes were equally as bad. They carried on towards the church and John started to add his thoughts into the equation;

'So, are we assuming that we are only looking for Jimmy in connection with both murders?'

'I think that is safe to say; yes. Unless you have a different idea?'

Due to the connection that had been established early on, between them as youngsters it had not been given any consideration that there might be two murderers in the area.

'Not really, Sir, it is just that with the hiding of the body and the hand being removed, it seems more premeditated than Steve being smashed about the head and left.'

'I agree with how you are thinking; though I think it highly unlikely. It is a possibility that the 2nd murder is different to muddy the waters. Also, I think it was left as it was at the tower so we would find it. Also, I can only hope we are correct as I do not like the thought of two maniacs running around.'

As they approached the church; the vicar came running towards the gate.

'I was just going to the vicarage to ring the police.'

'And you are?'

'Sorry Sir; this is Reverend John Tidy, the local vicar.'

Ray looked at the man standing in front of them; who was trying to catch his breath.

'Just take your time, Sir.'

As the man stood and slowly calmed down; the red flush on his face eased. Ray waited, but would not have been quite so patient if he realised the information he was about to receive; this was to be a slice of the luck they were waiting for. The Reverend starting speaking very quickly, as despite his many years of talking to parishioners about a multitude of subjects; he couldn't help but sound excited about his discovery.

'Sir, please slow down and tell us what you need to.'

John went on to explain that he needed to show them an old shed at the far end of the churchyard. Ray just could not help but have a good feeling about things, and seemed to get ahead of himself as well:

'John, get on the radio and arrange for a forensic team. Mr Tidy can you show me the shed.'

Ray and the vicar walked away while P.C. John Ford started things moving. As they walked towards the back of the church; Ray was thinking who was to blame for a shed not having been spotted the last time the teams had been at the church. As they approached, he realised why; the team had been concentrating on the church tower where Jeff had been discovered. The word shed was an overstatement; against the back wall of the church was an old structure that was covered in moss and weeds that was almost hidden from view. The vicar pointed at the building and Ray could see that at some point the moss had been pulled away and a very ramshackle door was slightly ajar.

'Okay, Sir; if you can just give me some space. I need to look inside.'

The vicar stepped forward and made to pull the door.

'NO, do not touch anything.'

The sharpness of his tone made John Tidy jump.

'Sorry about that but please just leave this to me.'

Cautiously Ray pulled and pushed against the moss and overgrown weeds to get the door open further. It was obvious that even if not very far, the door as it was had been opened recently. He pulled his mobile phone out of his pocket and switched on the torch; he was not too sure about what he had found but knew it was a breakthrough. Facing him was the upturned mess of what Jeff had been using as a makeshift bed; as he initially looked around at the shambles in front of him; his eyes were drawn to a dull glint of light. As he had moved his torch its light had caught the blade of a screwdriver. He carefully picked it up and dropped it into an evidence bag. As much as he knew he should wait for the forensic team to arrive, he found it difficult to control the urge to basically strip the place bare; not that looking around it would take much to do this. It was obvious that there was blood on the blade of the screwdriver. Fortunately, he got his emotions in check; when he saw the t-shirt with a stain on it and then the chisel.

Making a point to not touch or brush against anything; Ray backed out of the shed. John Ford looked at the evidence bag in his hand and couldn't help but smile as he realised the significance of the item contained within.

'The team will be busy when they arrive. Having a quick look around there is a stack of evidence to gather up.'

'Anything I can do to help, Sir.'

'Yes, you can go with the vicar to the vicarage and take a concise statement, mainly regarding anything he knows about this building.'

As he finished speaking Ray looked back at the shed. It looked so insignificant; anyone looking at it would not give it a moment's thought other than it was a storage place or even just an empty shell. As they both took another look at the place, that Ray was now hopeful would provide a lot of the answers they were looking for, Lisa and her team arrived.

'Morning, Lisa; some work to keep you busy for a while.'

Ray handed her the evidence bag and explained about the t-shirt and chisel. With Ray helping and now with the team onsite to gather evidence, they pulled the door open as far as it would go. Lisa took a look inside then turned back;

'Right, there is not a lot of room inside to work in, I think the easiest way forward is to form a chain. I will go inside and pass stuff out to be catalogued.'

Lisa looked to the others who had come with her,

'First let's get some light on the subject shall we.'

They placed some large lights and a generator at the edge of the door; trying to leave as much space as possible. Working methodically through, Ray watched as the team laid stuff out on a cloth as Lisa handed it down the line. As he stood watching he started to feel that slowly pieces were falling into place. Then he felt disappointed that after the initial pieces, there seemed little else to get excited about. It was mainly some stuff that he figured belonged to Jeff; he couldn't help but think how his mum would feel knowing her son who had been missing for some while was so close to home. As he started to think they had got as much as they were going to get; two things happened that lifted his mood.

His mobile phone rang; looking at the display he saw it was Tim calling; as he went to push the button to answer he saw Lisa standing in the doorway. She was holding an overcoat that he recognised as belonging to Steve; in her other hand was a spade. For a brief second, he was not sure what to do first, answer the call or speak to Lisa. In the end, he acknowledged with a nod to Lisa, then answered the phone.

'I think we have something, Sir.'

Tim couldn't keep the excitement out of his voice.

'I think you may be right, Tim.'

Tim had called as the information he had been given about where to look for the watch had proved very helpful. Expecting to pass this news on to the D.I. he was somewhat put out that there was other; seemingly more pressing information that the D.I was dealing with. Usually, Ray would listen to all his team, but he knew the importance of what Lisa held in her hands.

'Tim, you are going to have to wait and tell me when we all get back to the station.'

Before Tim could respond, Ray had hung up. He went over to Lisa.

'I take it we have now got some important pieces of the puzzle.'

'Certainly, would look that way.'

'If I can leave you here to finish up, then get the items back to your lab to test. Dare I ask can we get the results as soon as possible.'

There was no need for Lisa to answer; Ray was fully aware it would take time. He also knew that Lisa would work as quickly as possible.

Ray left the scene and quickly made the short walk back to his car. On his way back to the station he called through and sounding like a repeat message asked for everyone to be alerted to be back in the office immediately. He could not help but think there was now some light at the end of the tunnel; and they were making their way quickly towards it.

Chapter Fourteen

Ray made his way into the office; the atmosphere was buzzing with anticipation as to what the latest news was. The level of excitement had increased more; when Tim had entered and told the others as they returned about his call to Ray. In as much as they were keen to hear what Tim had obviously found out; the reaction he had received when calling suggested that Ray had even more interesting news. Due to everyone having been called back urgently; there was no sign of Adam; after his recent appearances at the briefings, Ray was not sure whether to be relieved or not.

He strode purposefully towards the front of the room; as he walked past people, they fell silent; it was almost as though no-one wanted to miss anything. The first thing when Ray spoke brought a noticeable groan from the others:

'Tim, what did you find out?'

Even Tim was surprised to be asked first.

'Mr Bloggs, and yes that is his real name. He was extremely helpful; once I put him straight on a few points of law and exactly why I needed to know about the watch.'

This brought some coughs from others; as even though they knew Tim could look after himself he was regarded as the quiet one of the team. The idea of him threatening someone was not the normal. Tim explained that once he had shown the pictures of both the watch and Jimmy; Mr Bloggs told him that yes just over a week ago the watch was brought in. He knew immediately; firstly, the value and secondly that it had not been passed down through the family; which was the story he had been told. Tim continued; but tried to keep things short as he could see that Ray was itching to speak. He told them that the guy had been offered a small sum for the watch, but after some haggling both parties had shaken hands on £200. The dealer knew he had still got a good deal; but could also tell that the seller was getting impatient and angry; to the point that he showed no interest in listening to the terms involved in returning for the item, Joe Bloggs couldn't help but see £ signs. To say he was visibly upset would be an understatement when Tim told him he was required to take the watch as evidence.

'That really is all I have, Sir.'

'Well done, Tim, it just gives us more to go on.'

Before Ray could continue; Sheila interrupted:

'Come on then, Sir; what was so important you called us all back at a moment's notice.'

Normally a member of the team interrupting like this would get a quick retort. Knowing what he had to say to them meant he just smiled. Ray went on to tell them about the discovery of the shed and the screwdriver. As he was talking the excitement in the room increased; those who had known him the longest knew there was more.

'After I found the screwdriver, I also saw a chisel. By this time Lisa and her team had arrived and started to strip the interior out. It soon became obvious that someone had been living there. Then the reason I cut your call short Tim happened. Lisa uncovered a spade and a coat which I expect to hear later; have traces of Steve's blood on them.'

Despite everyone in the room knowing they still needed to locate Jimmy Hammer; this really was a breakthrough in the case, and Ray could feel that it had given the team a boost. Everyone felt they were heading towards a conclusion of the case.

'I will go and pass this news onto Adam, and we are now waiting for forensics to do their stuff. But even I am expecting to hear that Jimmy's fingerprints are on everything we recovered and that unfortunately, the blood samples will be of both Jeff and Steve.'

Sheila was next to speak:

'So, with all this stuff found in the shed; are we assuming that Hammer is still in the vicinity?'

Before Ray could answer Tim spoke:

'The guy I spoke to said that the visitor we now know was Hammer arrived in a car; he also told him that he needed the money quickly as he had to visit a relative in the north.'

This brought another collective groan as all of a sudden, they thought their suspect could be miles away. Tim soon got their attention again though.

'Mr Bloggs got a make of car and despite him not having CCTV in his car park; there is a set of traffic cameras not too far away. I have already asked for the films from around the time he was visited by Jimmy. Hopefully, by the end of the day, we should have a registration to go on.'

'Well done again Tim. As soon as you get the films, I want everyone looking for the car.'

Ray left a room that was buzzing and went to see Adam. He was surprised to see Adam sitting behind his desk without his jacket on; in all the time they had worked together he could not remember a time seeing Adam not in full uniform.

'Sorry, if it is a bad time, Sir. I just wanted to update you.'

'That is alright, Inspector; I was just sitting reminiscing about my time here.'

'I thought you were looking forward to the move, Sir?'

'Do not misunderstand me; I am very excited about the future. That does not stop me from realising what has been a relatively good time in my career.'

As usual, Ray felt there was a wall between Adam and everyone else; even though he was moving on, he still felt that he had contributed a lot to the success of the force in recent years. Ray found this hard to take as he looked on Adam as an office policeman. With so much going on, and knowing he would not be in the position much longer; Ray decided not to say anything that would upset anyone.

Ray could see Adam start to bristle with pride again; as he brought him up to speed with everything that had happened in the last few hours. Adam even sat more upright; then stood up and replaced his jacket; smoothing down the sleeves and adjusting the buttons. Then as if to prove Ray's thoughts about him he said:

'That is good news; so, everything should be wrapped up nicely; ready for me to pass along the information to the division. It will also give a good start to my successor.'

All Ray could see if he stayed much longer was an argument developing, so he just bit his tongue and said:

'I will let you know more, as soon as I can, Sir.'

'Of course.'

As a footnote to end the conversation Ray added as he was leaving the room:

'It will not be immediately.'

He never heard the reply as he had already shut the door. Coincidentally Ray found it funny that as he walked back to his office, a young P.C he had not properly seen before approached him. He was holding an envelope:

'Excuse me, Sir; we are collecting for a leaving present for the Superintendent.'

As Ray had grown older and become more settled in recent times; he had also become more tactful. So, with no more than a quick acknowledgment he placed some money in the envelope. At the same time, he realised there would be a leaving party to attend as well. As he went back towards his office he called out:

'Any news from the people we need to hear from?'

Tim looked up from his desk:

'Nothing yet, Sir.'

Ray looked around at the team; and thought about the fact that currently even though it had been a productive day so far; they were now all really in a state of limbo. Apart from the possibility of someone spotting Jimmy, they were waiting for others to finish their work to allow them to move on.

'Right, unless any of you want to visit anywhere you think Jimmy is hiding. I suggest we call it a day. Be here tomorrow at 7am, and I think we are in for a busy day.'

Chapter Fifteen

Ray looked forward to the prospect of getting home at a reasonable time and enjoying the evening relaxing with Jenny. It just so happened that they arrived home within minutes of each other. They decided as they had the time; they would get ready and have an evening at the dance school. As usually happened during a case spare time became limited; this meant they had not been to a dance class for a couple of weeks, so both were looking forward to the chance to see the others. They had a quick meal and made the journey to the dance studio.

Despite the thoughts racing around in his head; Ray soon found the music and the company managed to push the thoughts to one side; he always remembered Carole telling them all as they started to learn, that the brain had compartments and the different steps for each dance were filed in a different area until you had learnt enough to mix the teaching together. He had found this pattern of thinking helped in other ways as well, and helped immensely in allowing him to relax when the chance arose. The things Ray found nice were that despite them not having been for a few weeks, everyone was pleased to see them again. Soon he was whisking Jenny around for a quickstep, and enjoying himself.

As usual, time flew past, and after learning new steps in the Argentine Tango and several more dances around the floor; it was the end of the evening. The other thing Ray found relaxing about being at the dance school; was despite that everyone else who came along, knew they were both police officers. No-one made a thing about asking what they were working on or how it was going, this allowed Ray to switch off for two hours in an evening. Having said their goodbyes and promising to get back again as soon as work allowed, they started the journey home.

Things had a tendency during an investigation; for things to happen without people being aware of it. As Ray and Jenny were driving home and chatting about the evening; then not being able to help themselves also talking about the case; one of these moments was taking place.

Also driving as, he thought of it as to home; Jimmy Hammer had made the decision at about the time Ray decided to go dancing, Jimmy decided to make his way back to Norfolk. Driving carefully so as not to attract any attention; he was unaware that at that moment film footage of him driving into the car park; where Joe Bloggs worked from was being passed by email to Tim Jarvis. Tim would see this first thing in the morning.

Jimmy knew he was taking a risk in coming back, and had heard on the car radio news about the work the police in King's Lynn were doing to investigate the two murders. Despite understanding the risk, he was confident enough that he could deal with it and still stay out of sight. Also. he did think he would be able to make decisions on what to do while on home territory; he found that as much as he had thought it fun to travel away from the area; he was happy to be approaching places he knew well. And for an unexplained reason, he was still of the mindset that he was getting away with things. Even allowing for the thought that he had got away with his latest crimes; Jimmy decided that he would return under the cover of darkness. Throughout his criminal life; darkness had been a friend. He had made his way back from the North East in no particular rush and had got back to the outskirts of Terrington once it was dark. One benefit for him was that like a lot of villages in the area; there were not a lot of street lights. Wanting to be as careful as possible he parked the car alongside some derelict warehouses; then making his way on foot he went across some fields and arrived at the back of the church. Suddenly when he saw the old shed it dawned on him that the police were more aware of things than he thought. Not knowing what had gone on, had been down to the police not releasing to the press the complete information of what had been found in the shed; there had also been no mention to anyone the details Tim had found out about the watch. Both sides of the people involved in the case would look at the press coverage differently. In the modern world of social media; news spread a lot quicker and a lot further nowadays. Fortunately for the police in the area, though sometimes frustratingly and despite Adam doing his best to give interesting press conferences, the local paper only appeared twice a week; also, the rural nature of the area meant gossip only spread so far. Therefore, this meant that even listening to the news Jimmy had not heard the full extent of the progress that had been made.

He didn't need to hear anything at the minute he saw the police tape across the front of the shed; also, the sight of the contents of the shed that had been decided were of no use were still laying on the ground at the side. Jimmy made his way more cautiously back to the car; being extra careful not to be seen. His mind was racing as he tried to think of his next move. Not in the same respect as the police involved; luck was to again play a part in the case. As he made his way back to the car and at one point changing his route; he saw the old building in the corner of a field. Even though his route had not been much different, he had not spotted the house due to it being surrounded by conifer trees. He approached carefully and could see that more windows were broken than were intact; but it had a roof and was out of the way. Using the torch on his phone and being careful to shield the light as much as possible; he made his way to the back of the house. The door was a sturdy one but even though it was in place Jimmy could see it had been forced several times by the look of it. Jimmy eased the door open slightly; but couldn't help but jump at the screech of the hinges. He soon realised there was no-one around to hear it; he made his way in and felt the urge to gag at the smell. Knowing he had no other choice currently he held his breath and made his way silently around. After having looked in all the rooms and seeing there was no one else there; he thought it was as good a place as any to wait for a few hours, he had no idea it was going to be longer than that and also would be the last place he would stay. One of the rooms upstairs didn't look as though it had been disturbed much, so he decided it would do him. Realising he would be best to only move around at night; he went back to the car and got some bits and pieces out to take with him; apart from thinking of the obvious of fingerprints and DNA there was nothing left in the car to link it to him; not wanting to draw attention to himself burning the car out was not an option. At the time as well, Jimmy was still thinking that he might still need the car, so quickly checking that it could not be seen from the road he left it where it was, then walked back to the place that was now home. As he sat against a wall having found some old blankets to sit on; he opened a can of beer and drank some while trying to get things straight in his head. Through all his life including the time spent in prison Jimmy had always been a positive person; there had been a short period of time during the last sentence he had suffered minor depression but was sure he had worked his way through this. As he sat quietly and alone, he started to find it difficult to see a positive way forward. Slowly as he continued drinking, having made sure earlier in his trip that he always had cans of beer in the car; Jimmy felt himself falling to sleep.

As Jimmy was wondering what to do next; Ray and Jenny were settling down having got home from the dance class. Ray was also wondering what to do next in getting the case solved. He was aware that Adam would like it all wrapped up; before he moved on. This had very little bearing on how Ray felt; he wanted the case solved quickly as a way of closure for the families of the victims. Steve's sister Jean had found it difficult at the house, and very quickly decided on things she wanted to keep, and with it agreed between her and Ray had appointed a solicitor to organise a house clearance, then move things along to eventually sell the house. Jean had then returned to Leeds; thanking Ray for his support and finally asking that he let her know the result of the case. Despite the seemingly dysfunctional side of the Roebuck family; Ray also wanted to be able to tell them what had happened to Jeff. In particular he felt that Brenda, Jeff's mum, deserved to know. Even though she was very overbearing in the family it was obvious there was a deep feeling of a mother's love. He could not help but worry that once it was settled Brenda would find it very difficult to deal with. At the present, moment, Ray had no idea that things were going to end up a lot worse for her.

After sorting some things out in the house; Ray and Jenny made their way to bed, with Ray knowing the alarm was going to ring soon ahead of what he felt was going to be a very busy day. Over the years Ray's sleep pattern had changed, sometimes when working a difficult case sleep had been a few hours grabbed at his desk. Due to being very settled in his life now, he found sleep was easier and usually he would not be disturbed until the ringing of the alarm. But as soon as he was awake; the case was on his mind. Jenny was still settling into her new role and had told him last night, that in her words she was doing community policing. It was a bit more than this in that she was visiting local businesses to get to know them. This was something that could always be helpful in solving crimes; when local knowledge was helpful. They both set off for work, with neither knowing when they would finish. Ray could not shake off the idea that it was going to be an important day.

Chapter Sixteen

Ray's journey in was a good one, so he felt that this was an omen for the day. He arrived in good time and felt relaxed about things. As he walked into the office it was a hive of activity. Phones were ringing and being answered; he could hear taps of fingers on keyboards as information was looked at and added on to computers. Tim was the first to speak:

'We have the footage from the traffic cameras; so are working through it now.'

'Let me know if you find anything.'

'Will do, it shouldn't take long; as we do have a time scale, we are looking for.'

Ray made his way to his desk and was met by Sheila, who had more news to add to the growing list of information.

'I spoke to an officer based in Scarborough last night.'

Ray could not help himself as he replied;

'Are you thinking of taking some holiday?'

'As much as I like that area Sir; not the thing on my mind at the moment. The officer I spoke to was a desk sergeant and we know how little they miss on everyday happenings.'

Sheila told Ray that the sergeant had rung her as he had seen the picture, that had been circulated as the investigation moved further afield. There had been a sighting of Jimmy at a bed and breakfast hotel on the edge of the town. This came about when a local and very eager crime reporter had seen the photo as part of a weekly press release. The reporter had used the picture in an article he wrote, and the owner of the B&B had called in having seen it in the paper.

'Do not let Adam know too much about the reporter's success, you know how he likes to tell me the press are our friends. We know he had funds from selling the watch, but they cannot last indefinitely. So where else has he got money from?'

'All I can think is knowing, the things we are finding out about him. Is from his criminal activities and being quite astute, it is possible he has a stash of money to draw on.'

'So, are we thinking he may still be on the East Coast somewhere?'

'The B&B owner told the police that he had checked out one day ago but had stayed for two nights.'

'We need to find his car; which with all the traffic cameras should prove easier than finding him has done. I do not relish the thought of some poor soul, having to trawl through road camera footage to spot him, but this may be needed.'

'We may have been slightly behind him; but have been lucky to get the reports coming in. So, we could strike it lucky with sightings of the car.'

Sheila knew it was going to take a large slice of luck, but felt she had to do her bit at keeping the positive attitude that was around the team at present.

'It does feel as though we are getting somewhere; at the same time, it is still frustrating. I feel as if I know Jimmy better than he does himself, and now I just want to be able to sit and ask him why?'

Sheila could understand exactly how Ray was feeling and knew that everybody involved was doing their best so that questions could be asked and then hopefully answered. Suddenly from the far side of the room, there was a shout; got him! One of the constables who had been drafted in to look at the film footage; stood up from the desk and for a brief moment did not seem to know who to talk to first. Tim helped him out, by going and looking at the image that was frozen in time on the screen. The picture was of an original version of a Mini; it was a grainy photo as the traffic camera shots invariably were. It did look as though the car had been cared for, suddenly there was a crowd of officers eagerly trying to get a look at the screen. Ray looked at Tim:

'Can you enlarge the image, so we can possibly see the driver clearly?'

Tim silently pressed a few buttons and for a moment they all held their breath. Then before their eyes, there was the image of the man they wanted to ask so many questions of. The only major difference to the picture that had been circulated, was the person they were looking at had a beard. It didn't stop any of them from knowing it was the right man.

'Can you let the footage run on a bit?'

Again, Tim never answered but just concentrated on the computer, within seconds they watched as the car drove silently along the stretch of road; they all could identify the area as the High Street in Sutton Bridge, then the car turned left into the car park at Joe Bloggs. It then disappeared from view. Tim went to stop the tape:

'No, Tim leave it a while.'

The room was in silence as they watched and none of them noticed Adam coming in. He was in the room expecting

142

to hear the latest from the morning briefing. As Adam was about to ask if they had finished watching whatever it was; Sheila said:

'There he is again.'

The Mini had been picked up by the camera as Jimmy drove out of the car park, and turned away from the direction he had arrived from. The car went out of sight of the camera.

'I reckon he was heading towards the A17, and that possibly explains him being sighted in Scarborough.'

'I think you might be right, Sheila.'

As Ray went to continue the phone rang, an officer picked up the call and said:

'Phone for you, Sir; it is the forensic team.'

'Put it through to my office please.'

As Ray moved across the room, he noticed Adam skirted the edge of the room and was following towards his office, he also could feel as though he was walking a path of anticipation; not just from himself in thinking what Lisa would have to tell him over the next few moments. Everyone has a sense of excitement now they had seen the sightings of the car; it had affected the whole room when they had seen the man at the wheel who was their main suspect. It had a different feel to previously when they had just had a prison photo to look at. Ray had noticed over the last few days that all of the team had become fixed in the idea that not only were they tracking a killer of one of their own; it was also the knowledge to them that there was no good reason why either Steve or Jeff had been murdered. Ray picked up the phone as he acknowledged Adam at the door of the office, he put the call on loudspeaker, as this would allow Adam to hear the conversation and save Ray bringing him up to speed on things:

'I have my fingers crossed for good news, Lisa.'

'I think you will be pleased. Just so you are aware I had a couple of my teamwork extra to get this information as quick as we did.'

'It is appreciated.'

Ray could sense Adam thinking what is this costing the force, he chose to ignore him and carried on speaking,

'So, what are we looking at?'

Lisa went on to say that the results so far; were only the initial reports, and it would take longer to confirm everything.

'I can tell you though that there were usable fingerprints on both the spade and the chisel. Both the sets match with Jimmy from the system. Carrying out separate tests, we discovered that the blood on the spade is a match for Steve and on the chisel matches Jeff. We will carry on with the other tests and I will get my full report to you as soon as I can.'

'Thank you.'

This was the only response Ray could give; with the personal connection with Steve, he was relieved to have this proof. He placed the phone down and looked up at Adam. He received just the response he expected:

'I am pleased that that was good news. Though I feel it is going to cost.'

Due to feeling positive about the case and knowing the future was without Adam, Ray could not keep the smile out of his voice as he replied:

'It will be part of the end budget, Sir; the good news is we now have definite proof of our killer.'

There really was no response to this that Adam could give as he knew Ray was correct, so left the room. Though he still managed to have the last word:

'You better find him quick then, hadn't you?'

Ray just let him go. He realised there was now a solid enough case being built, so when Jimmy was located; Ray would be ready to press ahead. He went back out into the main room and saw everyone was busy, he gave it a moment then spoke,

'Right, everyone; I knew it was going to be an important day.'

Ray went on to tell them all; the results of the tests from Lisa. This type of information was just what they wanted to hear, and Ray could feel the level of anticipation increase noticeably. Ray decided that as they all returned to the tasks in hand, despite his love, hate relationship with it; he would take the opportunity to deal with some of the paperwork that always seemed to arrive on his desk when his back was turned. A lot of what he had to deal with, just required his signature to complete a trail of red tape. This was nowadays required to be kept in an archive room somewhere; in case it was needed in the future. Usually, it would be an ambitious young solicitor, who would want access; with the thought that a miscarriage of justice had occurred. If they could prove this, it would invariably help their career; Ray was fully aware that in the past, there had been several appeal cases nationwide that had returned different verdicts to the original court hearings. Fortunately, none of these had happened in Norfolk; something that Ray was particularly proud of. Some of the miscarriages were down to honest mistakes, though it always made him grimace when he heard rumours of police officers not being totally honest in their work. This was the reason he had been concerned when D.C Sam Penn had first contacted him regarding Steve; having made plenty of enquiries and taking the time to look through the notebooks recovered from the house. Ray was happy that Steve had not been involved in anything untoward in his career, which could harm any court case into his murder.

Ray spent an hour tidying up his pile of paperwork and checking over email correspondence; during this time, he would hear the occasional call from one of the team, as they found a piece of information to add to the ever-increasing board. The whiteboard was getting busier all the time as bits were added to the timeline of how things had occurred. Sheila appeared at the doorway:

'I have just spoken to Scarborough Police again; they have formed a timeline of their own. A couple of the team have been studying camera footage in the area of the B&B.'

It appeared that they had noticed the same car in the street outside the B&B; it occasionally moved, then parked again. Having spoken to Sheila the officer confirmed it was the same car they were interested in. The footage they had showed that the car left the area 24 to 36 hours previously.

'So, it is a help but without trawling through hours of tape with no idea which direction to start looking in. We now have the choice to make an assumption, which I never like to do.'

'The assumption we are making is?'

'That there are two obvious thoughts. First, he has moved on and could be going anywhere, or he is now either being brave or silly and heading back this way.'

'So, any ideas which path we chose.'

'I am willing to stick my neck out and go with him returning here. Before you ask, I do not know why.'

The rest of the day passed quickly, with everyone busy. Ray had spoken to Tim and suggested they get as much camera footage as possible of the routes back from Scarborough. He was fully aware this would involve some of the team, spending their days looking at computer screens; he was also hopeful that it would prove rewarding. Ray decided as the afternoon wore on; that the best thing would be to start afresh in the morning. So, telling the team that Tim along with two PC's would study computer footage; he then gave the rest their tasks:

'I want the rest of you searching for this car. It is highly unlikely that Jimmy has changed it, so let us find it.'

With his knack for impeccable timing; just as most of them were getting ready to leave. Adam walked in to the office. He was dressed in full uniform looking for all the world as though he was off to attend a formal function.

'I would just like a quick word with you all.'

As much as people tried to cover it up; you could not help but hear the audible sighs around the room. As always Adam carried on as though it was expected:

'I just wanted to make an official announcement, that I will be leaving my current position in two weeks' time.'

With timing that would put many entertainers to shame, Adam paused just long enough for someone to ask a question. Tim obliged:

'Where are you off to, Sir?'

Adam reacted as though the question was a surprise.

'I am heading up a new department at headquarters.'

Ray thought to himself that he could almost physically see Adam bristling with pride.

'I do hope that this case will be wrapped up sufficiently, to allow you to attend a gathering I will arrange, this will allow me to say goodbye formally.'

Again, Ray thought typical Adam that even saying goodbye would be formal. Around the room, people started to murmur good luck as they got ready to leave. Adam took this in his stride as only he could.

'Detective Inspector Keane; may I have a word.'

Obviously, this conversation would take place in Adam's office as he had already started to move out of the door, Ray followed but did not feel he should rush as he had been summoned; so, made a point of saying goodbye to everyone first, then made his way to the office, wondering what was to come next. It was no real surprise that the following conversation could have happened anywhere, but by moving to his own office Adam was showing his feelings of rank being important.

'So, how close are we to clearing this case up?'

Ray felt aggrieved in two ways, firstly at the use of the word we, and also Adam had heard most of the conversations that had taken place today so knew exactly where they were up to. He decided to let any feelings of annoyance pass by:

'The team have made a great deal of progress, including finding footage of Jimmy Hammer in his car. As you are aware Lisa and the forensics team have confirmed fingerprints and blood types from the items found at the churchyard.'

It was as though Ray had just given Adam a list of items; with no praise for any of the team and the hard work; Adam just stood ramrod straight by his desk and said:

'Well, if someone could just find Jimmy Hammer, we can get it all sorted.'

It was only the fact that Adam had now confirmed he was leaving, that stopped Ray from reacting totally differently. He decided it was best to keep the peace, and not aggravate Adam unnecessarily, so making his way to the door he replied:

'I will make them all aware of the urgency, Sir.'

As on recent occasions, Ray did not hear the reply, as he was already back in the corridor and had pulled the door closed. Ray made his way out to the car, already looking forward to getting home.

None of the team were aware that they were going to locate Jimmy very soon.

Chapter Seventeen

While the team had been busy gathering seemingly endless pieces of information; though at the same time building a conclusive picture of events. Their suspect, which due to all the tests carried out by forensics was definitely Jimmy Hammer; was sat leaning against a wall, with a half-empty can of lager, in a building that looked ready to be demolished. The interesting fact was that he was not very far away from any of the people who wished to find him.

Jimmy was surprised by how settled he felt in the house; he had slowly under the cover of darkness brought some food and drink from the car and spent his time drinking. This was to be his problem in the end. The first day he had been very twitchy each time there was a noise outside; this had triggered memories of his first night many years ago in prison. Despite his confidence now; his first prison term had been a shock to his system. The day in court had been a day of delays, so once the judge had sentenced him; he had been transferred from the court hearing and arrived at prison in the early evening. Consequently, by the time he had been processed through the system, he was taken directly to a cell. As the cell door slammed shut behind him and the warden had told him lights out in an hour; reality hit home as to the situation he found himself in. That first night he slept fitfully; being jerked awake by every little noise. As daybreak arrived and the cell doors were unlocked; Jimmy made a conscious decision on how he was going to deal with things. Unfortunately for him now, the longer he sat around thinking and drinking did him no good at all.

Jimmy stayed indoors during daylight; only venturing out once it was dark. He didn't mind too much as a lot of the time as a criminal was working at night. Though eventually due to circumstances this would prove the catalyst of his problems. Despite the bravado that his character had always portrayed to others; over the recent years and in particular during the time spent in prison, Jimmy had suffered from depression. He thought that after an episode during his last sentence, that the prison doctor described it as minor depression, once he took some tablets; also, to show willingness to the authorities by agreeing to some counselling he could deal with things. Due to his lifestyle, Jimmy was inclined to not take much notice of doctors, especially the ones he encountered in prison. To him, this had just been part of working the system to suit, though unknowingly it was to play a big part in the rest of his life. Now having time to sit and think about things; he realised how he had changed over the years. Until recently he had always thought of himself as calm and calculated, but over the course of just about two weeks; he had suffered from a red mist of anger which resulted in both Steve and Jeff being murdered. In particular with the death of Jeff, it upset him to think about it.

On one of his trips out at night, he had managed by being aware of his surroundings to get a hot meal. As usual, he would say it was someone else's fault in that they had left a back door open. The occupant of the house had served a meal of chicken and chips up, then left the kitchen to answer a phone call. With all the speed and cunning that had earnt him respect from other criminals; Jimmy was in the house and out again with the plate of food, whilst no-one witnessed anything. Despite the food satisfying him; it also helped fuel the feeling of depression that was slowly creeping up on him. As after he had eaten it; his next thought was he had no idea when he would next eat hot food. Jimmy found he was sitting and thinking more and more about his life. Up until a few weeks ago; he would have said he had enjoyed himself. Having attended various sessions with so called professionals while inside; he had come to realise that ordinary people despised his sort. If anyone had been asked about him, they would have probably answered that he was simply a criminal who got what he deserved. The more he thought of things he was inclined to agree. As a person he was always willing to put forward the argument that even though he stole things he never hurt anybody; even in the odd moment he had been caught in the act and challenged; Jimmy would always leave empty-handed rather than fight. His actions recently had dispelled this idea; with no real explanation as to why he had killed either person; it led him to become more depressed.

He forced himself to think ahead as to what should be his next move; anyone looking in from the outside world would have thought this was obvious. Jimmy could not even bear to dwell on the thought of handing himself in. If he was to get caught, then it would be a different matter; he knew if this happened, he would just admit to everything. His next thought was would it be a good idea to leave the area on a permanent basis; he had been happy the few days he had been in hiding for. He soon realised though that in this day and age it would be no different to staying put, he would still spend his time looking over his shoulder. As another day turned to night; he was resigned to the idea of staying where he was for now. In the time he had been hiding out in the old house, he had not heard anyone coming near and had got used to the outside noises that had disturbed him the first night and day. He opened another can of beer and thought to himself; I am doing okay so had another drink.

As with most cases investigated by the police, stories of the people involved and affected by crime seemed to intertwine. In this instance; currently, the police were in a good mood with how they were building their case and there were a lot of positives for them to work on. Meanwhile, nearby Jimmy was slowly falling into a pit of depression which was about to play a big part in the next few hours.

Steve's sister Jean, had returned to Leeds and her life there. Eventually, as the grief settled her life would carry on as before. It appeared that the other person who was most affected was to be Brenda Roebuck. The loss of Jeff; even with him having been missing before, was proving to be too much for her. For most of her married life, her husband Tony had never been much support, initially this had not been a major problem. He had spent his working life on a farm and she understood it was hard work, whilst he did this, she ran the household. As time moved on, Brenda always felt she wanted more not necessarily in a material way; but just in the amount of attention she got. Jeff had arrived as a pleasant surprise in her life and she doted on him; it was no surprise to her that Tony had never really bonded with his son and would always tell people that the women smothered the boy. When

Jeff had disappeared, Tony had just seemed to accept the situation as a part of life. Even seeing the body of his son at the mortuary had not really made a difference to his feelings.

Since the discovery of his body and the knock on the door from the police; Brenda had felt as though she was living in a daze. She was not sleeping properly, even with the tablets that were prescribed by her doctor. She knew she was on her own and would get no support from Tony yet despite her lack of feelings towards him, she could not help but still make sure his life carried on with her looking after him. A little piece of this in her mind was that Tony would know she still cared for him, she still hoped that at some stage he would return the feelings, some of her friends had told her many times this would never happen though she would always insist her friends were wrong. One thing she had noticed was since the news had been received Tony had been spending even more time at the pub, and if he was not there drinking, he was sitting with a glass at home. He was fully aware she did not approve of this; as always, she never said anything, it was almost as though he just pushed things to see if she would respond. Despite her friends telling her this was a form of abuse, Brenda just carried on as she had always done. Personally, she had never seen the attraction of alcohol and saw no reason to change her opinion of this.

It was thinking about these friends that did give Brenda some strength, there was a small group of women in the village who along with herself, were on various committees of associations in the village. These groups were something that Brenda felt very strongly about, over the years this group of females had stuck together, they were all very similar in that they had high opinions of themselves, and also how life should be lived. Brenda remembered one occasion at a meeting when chatting over tea and cakes, they had all seemed totally aghast when she told them that Jeff had come home from junior school and asked what was a snob. When she asked why he said that some of the boys at school had told him that his mum was one. In the current climate of life, it was an old-fashioned view about the associations they ran; if they took time to look beyond themselves, they would see it was not the same as years gone by, this was confirmed by the dwindling numbers of people who attended the various meetings and events they all were proud to organise throughout the year. Brenda had noticed that some of the people she had on the committees even were hard pushed to be as optimistic about things as she was. Her answer was always no matter how few attended something the people there were important because they had turned up; and these were the people they should mix with. Over the last few weeks several of these friends had called at the house to offer sympathy, and despite Brenda not feeling like it several of them tried to encourage her to get out of the home to even attend a meeting. So far none of them had been successful with the 2nd matter; in her mind, it was not right to go anywhere at the moment and would certainly not be proper to attend a committee meeting.

The day so far had been no different to any day recently, Tony had gone off in the afternoon; having sat in the chair all morning. As usual, he had not made any mention of where he was going, though it was easy for her to guess. Brenda had spent the morning and part of the afternoon doing housework. Tony had reacted as he always did to this by shouting at her as to why she was cleaning again and how dirty could a house get with only the two of them there. This last comment always hurt the most as it was as if he was reminding her that Jeff would not be coming back. Even though she had become used to her own company; loneliness was always a feeling in the back of her mind; sometimes this would take a grip on her, that she always felt it was like a vice holding across her chest. If she was honest this was one of the reasons she had got so involved with the various groups over the years. It gave her a sense of purpose and helped control the lonely feelings. Her life had always been a ritual, that followed the same pattern each day; and again, Brenda felt this was important. So as with every other day, she could remember in her life; mid-afternoon she made a cup of coffee and sat with the drink and two biscuits, at the dining table with the radio on. Brenda had always enjoyed listening to music; and throughout her life there had been songs come along that she felt meant a lot to her. Unfortunately, that afternoon while sitting with her coffee and her thoughts; the radio station played a song that unknowingly to Brenda started a chain of events that would change everything.

The particular piece of music was special in that it was a song; she had often listened to when Jeff was a youngster and at the time it would always bring a smile to her face; as she thought of seeing Jeff running around the garden. Today all it did was bring a lump to her throat as it played with her emotions. Sitting quietly, it took her a moment to realise why her cheek was wet; then the tears took hold and her body shook with the feelings of hurt and anger that took control. She sat long after the song had finished; making sobbing noises as she felt the familiar feeling that her heart had been pulled apart. Suddenly she realised that time had rushed past;

despite all the mixed emotions running through her mind; the role of dutiful wife that she had always played so well, kicked in and she started to think that she would need to start to get dinner ready for Tony. It was as though she was working on automatic pilot; as she methodically moved around the kitchen, then as if she needed any more proof to herself that today was not a good day, she was brought back to tears when she looked and realised she had set the dining table with three places. This had happened a couple of times since the police had knocked on the door with news about Jeff, Tony had just made a casual remark; that she was going senile which of course had been no help at all.

As she looked up and out of the kitchen window; she saw it was getting dark; glancing at the clock she thought that dinner was ruined and that Tony had decided to make a night of it at the pub. The first time he had done this she was annoyed that he had not bothered to let her know; after a few times, she found it a relief, in that it meant she could spend time alone with her thoughts of Jeff. At no stage in this process had she expected to react as she was about to. It was as if anger took over her body and she had no control over her actions; in one movement and accompanied with a piercing scream; Brenda swept her arms across the table sending plates and glasses crashing to the floor. It was as if the last few weeks; added to the last time she had seen Jeff, just piled on top of her and she had no way of halting her actions.

Anyone entering the house immediately after Brenda had left; would wonder exactly what had taken place. Later when asked even Brenda could not fully explain what had happened, as she had no thoughts at the time or after as to what she was doing. Several medical people who would eventually be involved in examining her, all gave the opinion that Brenda had had a blankness of mind that meant she lost control; though also it was as if she was trying to clear the past away. Brenda had left the kitchen and gone from room to room like a tornado; sweeping ornaments and possessions to the floor. Finally, she had gone upstairs and after throwing all of Tony's clothes on the floor and even ripping some up, she ended up in Jeff's room. It was described in the police report it was as though she had demolished the complete room, pictures and pieces that she had lovingly dusted over the years since Jeff left were picked up and smashed to the floor. Her final act in the room was discovered by the police eventually as they attempted to understand things; it was a framed picture of Jeff and Jimmy that she found in a cupboard that had been taken at school. She had picked it up and with tears rolling down her face threw it with all her might towards the window.

With no idea of what she was doing; Brenda ran downstairs, she grabbed a coat and picked up her car keys that had been laying on the side for weeks. She ran out of the house not even bothering to shut the door, got into her car and drove off. As Brenda was driving away from the front of the house; Tony was walking unsteadily along the back path to the house. He expected to get a glare of annoyance from Brenda but also thinking I bet she still has got my dinner ready. Instead, he walked into a scene of devastation. At the same moment not far away, Jimmy was also unsteadily standing up having drunk more than he intended; thinking to himself I need to go out and see if I can get some food. Checking that no-one was around outside he made his way cautiously to the road.

Meanwhile, Brenda had pulled the car into the side of the road and after sitting sobbing for some while; shook herself back to the present. As quickly as the anger had risen, it subsided and even though she could not remember everything, some of it came back and she could not think about or believe what she had just done. Suddenly the old Brenda was back and she just knew she had to get home in case Tony came back. Brenda drove back out onto the road and was so set on getting home, did not realise that her lights were not on; not going fast she still gathered speed on the empty road. Jimmy trying to be aware of making sure no-one saw him, never looked to his right as he stepped off the path. He heard nothing more, but Brenda heard a loud thud as he hit the front of the car and fell into the path of the wheels running over him.

Chapter Eighteen

The majority of the people who are woken by the shrill ringing of a phone in the night; take a few minutes to realise what the noise is, and how to react. For a lot of them, it is an initial thought of at this time of night it must be bad news. For Ray after so long in the job it was no different from a ringing phone during the day. Even when just waking up he was alert to any problems he was to hear about as he answered the call; picking up the phone he had no idea this call was to change everything that he and the team had been working on. Ray never took much notice of the caller I.D number on the screen and answered as he always did:

'D.I. Ray Keane speaking.'

'Ray, it is Dave Hulme.'

Dave was the nighttime D.I. at the station and Ray had always got on well with him. He was also aware that Dave would not be calling unless it was important.

'What news have you to pass on; that you need to ring me at this ungodly hour.'

Dave laughed, to him the hour was natural, he had worked night shifts in the force for several years and found it normal, he was single so there was no family to disturb his sleep during the day. Ray was one of those officers who had never handled night shifts well; it was part of the job, especially for uniformed officers just starting out. Ray was very pleased as he progressed through the ranks, to have more choice about working hours.

'Sorry about the time, Ray. I just thought you would want to know, there has been an accident in Terrington St Clement. A person has been killed after being hit by a car.'

'I take it you know how busy I am at the moment; so, I am assuming there is more to this.'

'Yes, basically because of the people involved. The driver of the car was Brenda Roebuck, and the person she hit was Jimmy Hammer.'

If Ray was amazed by hearing the first name involved; he was totally shocked by the second name. If all this was correct, then how long had Jimmy been this close without any of them being aware. By now Jenny was fully awake and sat up in bed as Ray ended the call and told Dave he would see him soon. He got out of bed and washed and dressed while explaining to Jenny, the details of the call. He was soon on his way to King's Lynn and was relieved that due to the time of night or morning depending on opinion, traffic was light even though it would be classed as unnecessary he would not be averse to using blues and twos if it felt it was warranted. It was part of the very basic training that as a police driver you only used the lights and sirens during the night if really needed. Another call from Dave via his Bluetooth connection interrupted his thoughts and Ray automatically slowed down so he could concentrate. He was approaching the outskirts of the town and thought, the one thing he did not need was an accident of his own to deal with:

'Ray, I thought I would let you know that there are taking Jimmy's body to the mortuary.'

'What about Brenda?'

'That was going to be my next comment; she currently is refusing to go to the hospital, and is asking John Ford to just take her home as she has to look after Tony.'

After Ray had expressed his amazement that all she was worried about was her husband, who was of no use to her at all in ways that were needed. He then added that it was good that John was on the scene; so, he would go direct and meet them at the Roebuck's house. He diverted his journey at the roundabout to take the junction for the A17, adding to Dave:

'How come John Ford is at the scene?'

'You could think it fortunate, depending on your outlook. The accident if that is what it is; happened just outside his house.'

'Okay, Dave; I will deal with this, and let you get on. You could always ring Adam and pass on the news.'

Ray could not keep the smile out of his voice as he said this, and was not surprised by the reaction he got.

'I will allow you that pleasure; if you do not mind.'

Dave knew how Ray got on with Adam, and even though he would be as professional as always, he knew Ray would derive pleasure from waking Adam in the early hours.

As he made the short journey on what was a very quiet A17; Ray had time to digest the information the phone calls from Dave had provided. There was a lot to take in and think over; such as how long had Jimmy been in the area, he thought it cannot have been too long as surely, he would have been spotted. The next question was what had Brenda, who as far as they knew had not been out of the house in days, been doing in a car at this time of night; and was she aware of her actions. They already knew from recent conversations that she had not been coping well, along with little or no support from her husband. As he approached the junction for Terrington he decided it was as good a time as any to disturb Adam; the phone rang several times before a sleep disturbed voice answered;

'Good morning, Sir.'

'I would not call it morning yet, and if you are ringing it is certainly not a good morning either.'

'Sorry, Sir, I just wanted to let you know the latest.'

Ray explained as much as he knew so far and told Adam he was on his way to the scene.

'I will let you have more details later this morning.'

With no attempt to keep the sarcasm out of his voice he ended the call by adding:

'Sorry to have disturbed you.'

Ray had intended to go to the home of Brenda and Tony, but as he turned into the road that led to the church, he came across the scene of the accident. John was still there and appeared to have things under control. Ray parked and got out to survey the damage; looking at the front of the car it was difficult to see any damage. Ray looked up as John came around the car:

'It looks as though there has been minimal contact; so how come he is dead?'

'According to the paramedics who very swiftly were able to assess things, it looks as though he has been caught by the edge of the bonnet. The speed looks very slow, but he fell into the road and looks as if he hit his head; finally, the car wheels ran over him.'

'Is identity confirmed?'

'It is definitely Jimmy Hammer, Sir.'

'John if you can stay here, I will get Tim out to help you clear the scene once you can. I will get Sheila to meet me at the Roebucks.'

As Ray made the calls and waited for an answer, John told him that the first responder on the scene had taken Brenda home, as she flatly refused to go to hospital. Ray acknowledged with a nod as he spoke to Tim, then Sheila. Ray explained the situation to them both and organised for Tim to come over and liaise with John to eventually get the car removed and see if they could find any witnesses. He changed his mind on talking to Sheila about her attending the scene and decided to get W.P.C. Jill Addy to meet him at the house, Sheila would go into the station and oversee things there until the morning briefing, there would be a totally different feel to this meeting than there would have been two hours ago. After he was happy that all was in hand; he left the scene to go and see how Brenda was.

Ray got to the house and was not surprised to see the first responder vehicle still parked outside. In the living room, Brenda was slumped on the sofa and the only words that came to Ray's mind was she was a despairing shadow of the woman he had first met. The paramedic was kneeling in front of Brenda and was still making an effort to get her to the hospital. Through the sobbing that was shaking her entire body; occasional words could be understood and it was basically a wailing NO. Ray quickly took charge of the situation, though the paramedic was going above and beyond his remit, Ray could tell that he was wasting his time in trying to get Brenda to hospital. Meanwhile, Tony was sitting on the edge of the chair opposite and despite what Ray knew about the home life of the family, he looked as though he was in a state of shock.

'Mr Roebuck, a W.P.C will be here soon to stay with you for a while. I need you to contact your doctor, he will need to come and see your wife, especially as it is obvious, she does not want to go to hospital.'

For a moment there was no response and Ray even wondered if Tony had heard him speak. Ray was about to talk again when Tony stood up:

'I will call the doctor but also I don't understand what has happened in the house this evening. I came home from the pub; the house looks like a war zone and Brenda was not there. The next thing I know this guy brings her in, in this state and then you turn up.'

Ray realised then that Tony had no idea about the car accident, he also took a moment to look around the room and could see what Tony meant.

'At the minute, Sir; we are not sure ourselves as to events this evening. I hope Mrs Roebuck will be able to help us understand things; but obviously not at the moment. If your doctor can come and see her; they may be able to give her something to calm her down.'

Ray had spent enough time in his career, being around people who were in a state of shock. He had soon learnt to recognise the signs of when you were going to get useful information, or without being harsh would get nowhere. The paramedic who was still doing his best to calm Brenda down said:

'I am sorry but if she will not go to hospital, there is not a lot more I can do here.'

'Thank you, you can get off to your next shout if you want, we will have people here for the rest of the night. Her doctor is going to come over as well.'

He stood up and stretched his back out from kneeling for so long:

'With some luck, I might get a coffee before the next call out, you just never know in this job.'

Fortunately, from Ray's point of view; within minutes of the paramedic leaving both the doctor and Jill Addy arrived.

'Jill, can you stay in here with the doctor and Mrs Roebuck, Tony I need to talk to you, shall we go to the kitchen.'

As Tony got up and walked into the kitchen, Ray followed and saw what was meant by the statement about a war zone. The living room had got off lightly with just pieces being thrown to the floor, the kitchen was a scene of destruction.

'Tony, I need to ask is the rest of the house like this, this may help explain tonight.'

'I don't know, when I got home the front door was open and I just saw this mess.'

'Tony, I need you to show me the other rooms.'

Even though it was becoming obvious that someone, more than likely Brenda had, had some sort of breakdown. Ray did not feel he could leave Tony in the kitchen where it looked as though everything had been destroyed, he still had not explained to Tony where they had found Brenda and felt that it could prove too much even for him. They proceeded to go to the other rooms in the house each seeming to have been rampaged but not on the scale of the kitchen until they reached the room that Tony said had been Jeff's. If it was possible then this room was even more ruined than the kitchen. Tony went even whiter than he had been as he stood in the doorway and spoke so quietly Ray struggled to hear him:

'This room was her shrine to Jeff; I can't believe she did this.'

He made a move to go in, Ray put an arm across his chest to stop him:

'Tony, please just let me have a look first.'

As Ray made his way around the room, he could see that nothing had been left untouched. By the window, he found the smashed photo frame. He picked up the picture carefully and could see immediately who was in it. He could only imagine that if this was Brenda who had done all this damage before driving off, then her state of mind must have been all over the place. They made their way back to the living room, where the doctor had got Brenda calmer in that her breathing had settled. He told Ray that he had given her a sedative and she would sleep for a while. Despite his frustration in wanting to know exactly what had happened; he realised that basically the case had reached a conclusion in a slightly unsatisfactory way. Waiting a few hours for Brenda to help them would not hurt.

'That is fine; thank you, doctor. Jill, it is a mess, but I need you to stay here so when Brenda wakes up you can talk to her and also let me know.'

He wanted to add that she should keep an eye on Tony as well; though he did not think for a moment the sentiment would be appreciated. Jill as always settled into her role; she spoke to Tony who responded as though on automatic pilot:

'Mr Roebuck, would you like a cup of tea?'

His answer seemed to suggest that even in shock he could be abrupt:

'Good luck with that, if you can find an unbroken mug let me know.'

He promptly picked up a bottle of whisky from the side of the cushion on the chair and took a large swig. Ray knew that Jill would deal with the situation with ease, so went to leave; to return to the station. He turned to say goodbye to Brenda and realised she was already sleeping. On his way to the station, he rang Jenny to let her know what had happened and to tell her he loved her.

Chapter Nineteen

During the short journey to King's Lynn, and what he knew would be a noisy and excited room, full of the team who would all be waiting to hear the latest developments. The pieces they already knew would be enough to them to signal the end of the case; Ray could not help but think about things. All he could come up with was unanswered questions; the outline was fairly straightforward; Jimmy had murdered Steve; following which for some unknown reason he had then killed Jeff. Then he left the area with no idea to them of when he had returned and managed to stay out of sight. Then that evening he had been out on the streets and by a twist of fate been run over by Brenda. As to whether this was deliberate or not remained to be seen.

As he entered the room, he realised he had been correct on one point; he did not think he could recall the C.I.D room ever being this noisy. In every corner of the room, there were pockets of the team all surmising about the events that had taken place. Ray made his way to the front of the room and commanded silence as soon as he said;

'Good morning, everyone.'

The only person missing was Adam; Ray knew this was a point-scoring effort as Adam would expect Ray to report to him on an individual basis after the briefing. Ray could already imagine Adam sitting at his desk, composing what he would say to the press and how he could make himself look part of the team who had solved the crimes. He would also want to keep the reporters interested as he made his announcement about his move to headquarters.

'I know you are all waiting to hear the details of last night. Currently, as most of you are aware all I can say is Jimmy Hammer was hit by a car and killed.

A voice from the back of the room, that Ray recognised as one of the P. C's who had been helping look at the road camera footage asked:

'Is it true, Jeff's mum was the driver?'

'Yes, it is but until I speak to her later, no-one is to mention that to the outside world.'

Ray then took the room through all he knew so far as to the events that led to the death of Jimmy. And told them he still wanted things tidying up as was necessary.

'Sheila will be in the office today; all enquiries direct them to her.'

He informed the team, that he would be going to see Adam; followed by the post mortem on Jimmy once Graham let him know a time. Finally, he would be returning to Terrington to speak to Brenda.

'I hope my conversation with her, will clear up a lot of loose ends.'

Ray left the room to go to see Adam, as he left them all to it, the noticeable difference to the atmosphere in the room; even though that basically the case was solved there was no real sense of congratulations amongst the team. Ray could fully understand the feelings and hoped that as they concluded things, they would all realise that their hard work had been worth it. He made his way upstairs to Adam's office and was told that he was expected; Adam was sat bolt upright behind his oak desk, with no indication that he had been disturbed in the early hours. As usual, his uniform was pristine and Ray could imagine the notes, he had been making in preparation to face the press.

'Good morning, D.I Keane. A good result for you in the end.'

'I am sorry, Sir; I find it difficult to think of it as such.'

It was almost as if Adam had not heard him as he carried on speaking:

'I suppose it could be called a form of poetic justice; that solves the case.'

For the first time since he had heard the news of Adam leaving; Ray thought to himself that he was not going to miss him.

'I can assure you, Sir; none of the team are looking at it like that.'

'I realise that; but with the evidence you had already gathered it is case solved, is it not?'

'Until I speak to Mrs Roebuck; I am willing to accept that our murderer has now been killed.'

'You surely are not suggesting it was deliberate on her part, are you?'

'That is the last thought in my mind; though I do need to get a clear picture of the events. I hope by the end of today it will all be known.'

Ray could not help himself but add:

'All in time for you, to give the press what they want.'

'You have never accepted how much help the press can be, have you.'

'I do understand Sir; it is just that as much as they help; it always seems they are quicker to criticise.'

Ray could tell the meeting was over as Adam spoke:

'I will let you get on; keep me informed throughout the day.'

Ray left the room with feelings of frustration. He stopped himself from slamming the door behind him by thinking, soon Adam would not be sat in that room anymore.

As seemed the usual course of events towards the end of a case; things moved very quickly. As he walked back in to C.I.D several of the team went to speak at once. Tim and Sheila both had information to pass on. Ray gave them a minute to sort themselves out then said:

'Sheila, you go first.'

'I have just had a call from the mortuary. The post mortem will be at 12 o'clock.'

Tim commented:

'That will be good. Get it out of the way before lunch.'

Ray smiled at them both, then looked at Tim.

'So, what news do you have?'

'I think we may have found Jimmy's car. A local farmer rang in; he was driving into one of his fields this morning and noticed a car parked out of the way behind some sheds.'

'It is a shame; it was not spotted sooner.'

'The farmer who rang; said it was the first time he had been in that field this year; so, it would have been a good hiding place.'

'Okay, Tim you get over to Terrington, speak to the farmer. Then arrange to get the car back here. I am going to

172

see Brenda Roebuck and hopefully piece together last night's events.'

Ray looked around the room; and asked the P.C who had spoken up earlier from behind his computer, his name.

'It is P.C Dan Carol Sir.'

'Right, you can meet me at the mortuary for the post mortem.'

Ray knew from the look he got as a response that it would be the young P. C's first visit to the mortuary. Ray had always liked to encourage everyone to attend a post mortem; he always felt it went better for them if he was there to support them on their first one. The answer that came back was only just audible in the room.

'Okay, Sir.'

This led to several minutes of banter from several of the others; who had all been in the position themselves. One of the quips was to be expected:

'Wait until afterwards, before you have lunch.'

Ray was happy to allow a few moments of humour then quickly quietened the room down;

'Right, you all have work to get done; so be back here at 4.'

Ray left them all to get on; and made his way out to the car and the journey to Terrington. He was hopeful that if Brenda had been able to snatch a few hours' sleep with the help of the tablets from the doctor; she would now be in a position to be able to tell him exactly what had happened. His own thoughts and hopes were that it had been a terrible accident; he could not imagine Brenda doing it deliberately. Also, as no-one had reported seeing Jimmy about, then there was no way she could have known he was in the area. As much as it was not the result he would have liked; he had to agree with Adam, that it could be looked at as a form of poetic justice. Though he could not help but feel that Brenda would suffer the consequences of the evening for years to come. Ray pulled up outside the house and was disappointed to see one of the local press reporters waiting outside.

'D.I. Keane, what is the latest news?'

'You can wait along with all the others, until the press conference later.'

Over the years despite all Adam said, Ray had managed to become very adept at being able to walk past reporters without any problems of pushing and shoving. He was able to do this again by walking down the front path while answering the question; also making a point of shutting the gate noisily, this then acted as a barrier. W.P.C Jill Addy had heard the car pull up and was waiting with the door open, Ray said nothing until he was inside with the door closed:

'Morning again, Jill; how is Mrs Roebuck doing?'

'Not sure, how to answer that one Sir. She has managed to sleep; due to the sedative, the doctor gave her. She woke about 15 minutes ago and has just sat weeping.'

Ray walked into the living room, seeing Tony Roebuck sat in the chair as he had been the previous time;

'Good morning, Mr Roebuck.'

As he had come to expect, all he received as way of acknowledgement was a grunt.

'Jill, if you have been able to tidy the kitchen, can you make some tea; while I talk to Mrs Roebuck.'

Ray did notice that it looked as though Jill had tried to help by tidying up some of the mess, that had been left the previous evening. Jill made her way to the kitchen, then surprisingly Tony spoke:

'I don't know what she thought she was doing, going off in the car like that.'

Ray found it interesting that he only mentioned the car, and said nothing about the mess that had obviously been caused by her before she left. He did not want to start a discussion with Tony, as he did not want anything, she may hear to influence Brenda's recollection of events.

'I will just sit and talk to your wife for a moment if that is alright.'

Tony reverted to type and grunted as he left the room. Ray sat at the opposite end of the sofa to Brenda and turned towards her. He wanted to avoid it appearing like a formal interview, as he felt he would get more information if she could stay relaxed.

'How are you feeling now, Mrs Roebuck?'

He realised as he asked this, that it was a mundane question as to anyone the answer would be obvious. He was therefore taken aback when she first spoke:

'I am not too bad.' Then as if she realised, she was talking, she quickly carried on:

'I cannot stop hearing the thud, as his body hit the front of the car. I never saw him, one moment there was nothing, then he was on the road.'

'I am sorry to have to ask these questions, do you know how fast you were travelling?'

Ray already had an idea of the answer, as the traffic accident team had been out and estimated that the car was travelling no faster than 30 mph.

'I was going at about 25 mph; it is a 30mph speed limit.'

Her tone of voice took Ray by surprise, it was as if the fact of everything that had happened in the previous hours; did not really matter. Though him suggesting she might have been speeding seemed unbelievable.

'I have never broken a speed limit in my life, they are surely in place for a reason.'

Ray could only put this sort of response down to shock, so decided to carry on the conversation.

'So, where had you been; when you went out?'

'I had been nowhere in particular; I just had an overwhelming feeling to get out of the house. Now I wish I had stayed indoors.'

Brenda started to sniffle, and Ray could see tears starting to form; he was aware he did not want to upset her any more than necessary though he needed to get as much information as quickly as possible.

'In your own time; can you tell me what happened, firstly in the rooms in the house then when you went out.'

Brenda looked up and seemingly noticed the broken ornaments for the first time. Ray slowly spoke and told her that it looked as though every room in the house had suffered some devastation.

Brenda took a deep breath as though knowing what she said next would upset her.

'I cannot remember much, from before I was in the car. I went out for a drive. After a short time of driving aimlessly around, I parked near the cricket field. Time seemed to pass quickly, and I decided I had to get home for Tony. As I pulled away and drove down the road, I saw a shadow at the side of the car; then heard the thud. The next thing I was properly aware of was John Ford crouching at the window of the car and helping me out.'

Ray soon realised while listening that all that had happened was a terrible accident and Brenda would live with it for the rest of her life. It was as though she had blanked out the damage that she had done to the house before leaving, this again could be down to shock. He knew she would get little in the way of support from her husband, though he hoped her friends and the doctors could help. He could see that sitting and reliving events had exhausted her; he knew that he had all he needed for now. If the results of the post-mortem, were as expected, then he would be recommending that no further action be required. Looking at her features; Ray knew that the one last question he had for her could easily tip her over the edge again, even though he thought it would be better if the doctor was there. He really wanted to deal with as much as possible in the visit. Taking a deep breath,

'Brenda, do you know who you hit last night?'

Her reaction was immediate, what little colour there was in her face drained away and tears started to flow down her cheeks. Ray knew he had to continue and get this finished up; fortunately, Jill chose the moment to come back in the room, Ray moved so she could sit next to Brenda. Through the tears she replied:

'Yes, it was Jimmy; wasn't it.'

Before he could say anymore; her body was shaking as she wailed into the shoulder of Jill. He knew he had all he was going to get now, he acknowledged that he was leaving; Jill looked up and said:

'The doctor mentioned that he would be back in later this morning, Sir.'

Ray's only thought was it was going to be needed; then made his way out of the house, knowing that next, he had to meet Dan Carol at the mortuary. He still had the obstacle to pass that was the reporter who had now been joined by another; he gave them no opportunity to speak:

'Still no comment, gentlemen.'

Ray was in the car and the door closed before they could respond. On his way to the mortuary, he rang Sheila, to find out the latest from the station. She told him that Tim had been to Terrington and they had recovered Jimmy's car from behind an old warehouse; the forensic team was making a start to go over it. Tim had already noticed some pieces in it that confirmed Jimmy had been using it.

'How was Mrs Roebuck?'

'Confused to a point, is the best way I can describe her.'

Ray went on to tell her all that he had found out; she agreed with him that it sounded as though it had been a terrible accident, with the added cruel twist of fate.

'I will see you after the P.M.'

Ray pulled into a parking spot outside the mortuary, it was part of the hospital, but Ray always felt it was a well disguised building that did not draw attention to itself. He looked up and saw Dan Carol was waiting outside the door. He looked at the young P.C's face, and could not help but smile, as he realised the man was looking pale already. Ray walked up to him,

'Come on then young man; let us get this out of the way.'

The reply followed a large gulp of air,

'Certainly, Sir.'

They walked in and as always, the first person they saw was Dennis the assistant. As he usually seemed to be doing, he was eating; this time it was a chocolate bar, he offered both a piece, being fully aware they would refuse.

'Morning Ray, you have brought another lamb to slaughter then.'

Dennis laughed as he spoke.

'Play nicely, Dennis, I never understand how you always spot them at their first experience.'

'Might have something to do with them, looking as white as our clients and the sheets they are wrapped in. Graham is ready for you.'

Despite the banter from Dennis, Ray had respect for all the team who worked in the mortuary, and Dennis was always on hand if it became too much for any of them. Dennis gave them the regulation gowns and face masks, then led them through the double doors. As with everyone who stepped into the room for the first time, Dan was amazed by how clean and bright everywhere was. The overhead lights seemed to reflect off every surface and briefly dazzled his eyesight.

'Who is this you have brought with you?'

'Graham, meet P.C Dan Carol, and before you ask yes this is his first.'

'Well, it will be a nice straightforward one; to break him in gently. I decided as it is a fairly standard examination, I would make a start to save you time.'

Ray noticed that Dan had not taken his eyes of the body since they had stepped in the room; he was impressed that he appeared to be taking everything in. He left Dan to his own thoughts.

'So, Graham, what do you have for us?'

'He died very quickly and the alcohol levels in his body suggest he would have known very little about it. The glancing blow from the car threw him into the road, he cracked his skull on the tarmac, this is definitely the cause of death. The injuries he sustained from the car running over him just compounded things.'

At this point, they all heard Dan take a deep breath as Graham pointed into the cavity that had been Jimmy's chest.

'If you look you can see his broken ribs and several internal organs have been crushed.'

'I think we can take your word for that. So, basically, you are saying his death was an accident.'

'I think so, having been shown pictures of the car; there is no major damage, that shows there was great speed or intention.'

'Thanks, Graham, if you can get me your full report as soon as possible. We can then wrap things up.'

Dennis who never missed an opportunity of having some fun at the expense of young officers spoke next,

'Maybe you would like to see the damage to the brain from the impact with the road.'

Ray was not sure if Dan was trying to impress or not, he stepped forward saying,

'Might as well do,'

Ray put his arm out, with Dan having done so well so far, he saw no reason to spoil things; he also had a good idea of the mess the brain would be in from having bounced around inside the skull.

'That is fine Dennis, but no need for that.'

They left the room in silence and Dennis started his job which was to tidy up the body, usually, this was to make it ready for a relative to view. In this instance, Ray knew of nobody to notify. Jimmy would have a simple service at the local crematorium. There would be an announcement in the local press, so there may be a few people attend. He turned to Graham and Dan.

'So, as much as it is not the result I hoped for, in a way it is karma that Steve Edwards was smashed in the skull to kill him, then his killer dies smashing his skull.'

The others knew Ray was just expressing his thoughts, so instead of answering they both nodded.

'Thanks, Graham, I am sure Dan enjoyed his first experience of your workplace; he managed to stay standing all the way through, so that is a good sign. Now Dan are you ready for lunch?'

Dan was slow to reply, though this did not surprise Ray.

'I think just a cup of coffee will do for now, Sir.'

Ray knew it was time for them to get going so said goodbye to Graham, and they made their way outside. After the bright lights in the mortuary, the sunshine from low in the sky seemed dull by comparison.

'I will see you back at the station Dan; there are loose ends we now need to tie up.'

'Okay, Sir, am I to stay helping for now.'

'Certainly, Dan; I have been impressed with your work, so you can see things through.'

Back in the C.I.D office, it was a hive of activity; the atmosphere was tempered by the feeling that a murderer had not been brought to court, though the case was solved. Ray moved to the front of the room and cleared his throat, as usual, this brought a hush to proceedings.

'Okay, team; I know how you are feeling; firstly, well done on a good effort as always.'

Tim spoke up,

'What is to happen to Mrs Roebuck, as surely it was an accident?'

'I am waiting to hear from the Crown Prosecution Service, though it has been recommended no action needs to be taken, as the death of Jimmy was an accident. She may well lose her licence, but having seen her today, I do not think she will be in any hurry to drive again.'

There were murmurings from several in the room along the lines of she deserves a medal, Ray picked up on this so added,

'Thoughts like that need to be kept to yourselves.'

Ray wanted to get things wrapped up so continued,

'Right, I know you will all want to get home and spruce yourselves up for the Superintendents leaving do.'

This brought some much-needed laughter to the room,

'Just a word of caution; before you, all start to cheer; remember better the devil you know. Prior to his party the Superintendent has one last press conference to give, he is going to finish it up, by announcing his move to them. So, get home as soon as you can then enjoy the evening.

Chapter Twenty

Ray had rung Jenny and they had arranged that she would travel up after work, he would get changed in his office and then they would attend the party. Even though this meant two cars being used it was easier as that morning Ray had had no idea how his day was going to go. As things had turned out, they had finished up as much as they had been able to by early afternoon. Having sent everyone home; Ray made his way to see Adam, he found that he had mixed feelings about the coming evening, especially as he realised this would be the last time he would be going into this office to brief Adam on the situation. Ray was fully aware that it was not going to impact much on his role at the station, with Adam moving on, though he found it a sobering thought that it was the end of an era. Despite their many differences over the years, invariably around conversations concerning finances, Ray had always been sure in his mind that himself and the rest of the team had the support of Adam. Ray walked in the door of the outer office and saw Natasha was busy tidying things up. If it was possible to surprise him anymore today, then Natasha did when Ray asked was, she looking forward to working with a new Superintendent.

'I am leaving today as well.'

Ray had not given the situation of Natasha much thought, she had been at the station since he first arrived.

'I have decided that it is a good time to go, and the replacement can bring their own team and ideas in.'

'Well, good luck with the future.'

'I am looking forward to spending time in the garden, and weekends visiting family.'

Ray smiled, then knocked and entered before Adam could say come in.

'A good result Inspector.'

'In a way yes, Sir. Are you ready for this evening?'

'I think so, though I feel it will be both a happy and sad occasion.'

Ray did not feel there was any need to reply to this comment. The surprises of the day continued when Adam next spoke:

'I think you should join me, at the press conference later.'

Adam had usually done his upmost to keep Ray and the press apart, so again he was confused at this comment.

'If you think it is a good idea, Sir.'

'Yes, I do; so, get yourself ready to face the cameras.'

Ray was always dressed smart, he just saw no pleasure in wearing a dress uniform for everyday work, he had no plans to put one on for this either.

'Okay Sir, I shall go and get sorted, and see you in time for your announcement.'

Ray smiled as he was now getting good at commenting as he left the office, so never completely heard any reply. He now had two things to attend; neither that he would say he was looking forward too. He had no idea why Adam would want him at the press conference, and several of his colleagues would say he would only be at the leaving party to make sure Adam went, and did not change his mind.

When he got back to the office, the C.I.D room was eerily quiet after the last few days and weeks. Ray sat quietly in his office and contemplated how this last case had played out. He was disappointed that he could not tell Jean that the man who had killed her brother would not face justice and that Brenda now had two reasons to struggle through for a long time ahead. Then he had a positive thought that at least the killer was no longer roaming around. There was going to be a busy day tomorrow with making sure everything was right on paper to explain their actions during the case. He would ring Jean in the morning to let her know what had happened; he was also going to contact a specialist group he knew about, that could possibly help Brenda moving forward.

Suddenly he could feel someone looking at him; he looked up to see Jenny stood in the doorway. Something he had come to quickly realise; was no matter how his day had been seeing her smile was guaranteed to make him feel better. This had taken some time to happen when they met as he had always felt his job was the most important thing there was. Ray had always tried not to have regrets about the past, he still did not but Jenny had helped him see that he had as much right as others to be happy. She had always told him, that he was good at his job but was also entitled to a life as well.

'I hear you need to be smart to face, your friends from the press soon.'

'Good to know the bush telegraph, still works as well as ever.'

'The desk sergeant took great pleasure in telling me as soon as I walked through the door. They all know your feelings regarding that side of the job.'

'I suppose I better get ready; you do know that Adam is also using this press conference to announce his move.'

Jenny stepped nearer and gave him a kiss:

'I understand also that the case has been wrapped up, even though not as you hoped. Congratulations anyway, I will leave you to get ready. Then we can go to the party and that will be that.'

Jenny left him alone and he made his way to the restrooms, having decided a wash and shave would suffice for the press and the evening event. As always there was a suit hanging in his office which he would change into. Already he was looking forward to the end of the evening.

As they entered the room set up for the press conference, Ray was amazed by how many people were there. News had obviously spread about the conclusion of the case, and all the media seemed to want to hear things direct. He took a seat at the end of the table, as this kept him out of direct sight, he looked up and saw Jenny standing at the back of the room. The conference followed a similar pattern to hundreds of other press briefings had done, Ray had attended a few but usually avoided them. He had to admit that sat there he could see that Adam knew how to work the reporters. He first made a short statement that outlined the events of the last 24 hours; before any of the press had time to ask questions regarding the details of the car accident, he had moved things along and the flow of the conversation was on how hard the team had worked, which ultimately led them to Jimmy Hammer. Once he was happy with things, Adam opened the conference up for questions he was clever enough to know the right time to do this. One of the reporters who Ray did not recognise and by his question indicated he was not local asked,

'What will happen to the driver of the car, that killed Jimmy.

Ray went to answer without keeping the sharp tone out of his voice by starting with,

'The driver has a name,'

He was cut off by Adam speaking,

'Mrs Roebuck, who unfortunately lost her son to the killer was driving. It has been investigated and will continue to be so, though currently no further action will be taken as it was an accident. Let us not forget what Jimmy had done before this terrible incident.'

This appeared to keep the press happy, Adam then took Ray by surprise by continuing,

'I also want to add my thanks to D.I Keane, for all the work he did on what was a very trying and personal case.'

Suddenly, Ray was having to deal with questions from all parts of the room, mainly focused on how he felt about the result of the case. Fortunately, after a few brief answers, he was saved from any more questions as Adam seemed to decide that was enough and took over again,

'Ladies and Gentlemen, I also want to take this opportunity to pass on some other news.'

This quietened the room immediately; Adam carried to tell them about his promotion, even though it was just a move to a different office. This led to another round of shouted questions which Adam was more than happy to deal with, so Ray surreptitiously made a gentle exit without anyone noticing. As he walked out of the room and along the corridor, he could hear Adam answering the questions and could also imagine him sitting there with his chest out bursting with pride. Keeping the press sweet was never something Ray considered in his daily routine. Jenny met up with him again and helped ease any tension he was feeling, by putting her arm around him and saying,

'Shall we go and get a drink; before we face the party?'

'What a great idea; I feel I may need several drinks to get through this evening.'

'If that is the case then, we may be better to book a hotel room, rather than arguing over who is going to drive.'

This was an easy solution as they had both learnt early in their careers to carry a spare set of clothes in an overnight bag in the cars. As they walked to a nearby pub; Ray called a local hotel in the town and made a reservation. They enjoyed their drink and then grudgingly on his part made their way to the party. It was being held in a local club, which the police used a lot for functions. It was a weird feeling for Ray as the last time he had been here was for the retirement party for Steve. In his mind, this was a bit of a nothing party, as Adam was not retiring and was going to be working at the county headquarters, which were only an hour away. On arriving and seeing that everyone was there he put on his best smile and decided he would enjoy the evening no matter what. One of the nice parts of the evening were all the team were able to see Jenny again, and conversations soon started up with them all wanting to know how she was doing. Ray had to admit as time passed, the evening did not seem to be too bad, he just was not sure about things and could not relax when Adam stood up at the front and called for quiet. Initially, Ray sat listening as Adam started to speak, as he continued though

Ray could feel himself start to cringe. It would sound to an outsider that in his time at the station. Adam had pulled things around and the success of all the officers was down to him. If anything was going to encourage Ray to have another drink then this was it, depending on the people involved it could be fortunate or unfortunate that Ray did not get a drink; before Tim who had sneaked outside for a moment came back in to talk to him. Ray could see Adam, looking annoyed this caused him to smile inwardly that even on his last day he managed to annoy Adam. He could also sense others starting to look at him as he touched Jenny on the arm and whispered quietly to her before leaving the table to go with Tim.

'I suppose I should thank you for giving me an excuse to leave. Though I do feel it better be a good reason.'

'That is going to depend on how you define good reason, Sir. The desk sergeant rang me; he tried your phone but got no answer.'

Ray reached in his pocket and realised that he had put his phone on silent for the press conference.

'So, what did he want?'

'A local farmer at Sutton Bridge, name of Chris Small. He was making use of the good weather to finish some harvesting off, even though a combine is a beast of a machine, as he was going through the field, he felt then heard something.'

Ray already had a horrible feeling where this was going but still felt compelled to ask,

'What caused this noise.'

'No-one is really sure yet, but it sounds as though it is a distinct possibility that there are human arms and legs in the back of a trailer and more remains in the field.'

'Why did we get the call?'

'The local police were informed Sir, but they feel it is something too much for them to deal with. Even though it is Lincolnshire we are the nearest big station.'

'Well, this is really going to finish the party off nicely, text me the address and I will make my way there. Can you tell Jenny I will ring her soon, then just for now get Sheila and follow me over.'

As an afterthought, Ray then added,

'Just tell Adam I have work to do.'

Ray left at a run with his thoughts already on his next case.